I0555757

NO DAY LIKE TODAY

AMY TEEGAN

5:10am Marshall

MARSHALL PAGE LIES on his side, blankets bunched up around his shoulders and tucked under his chin. As he slowly wakes up, he remembers that for once he actually has plans today.

I gotta get up. I gotta get moving, he thinks, rubbing the sleep from his eyes. *I gotta get ready. Today is going to be a great day.* Today will be the best part of his week. His month.

As he steels himself, coaxing his old muscles to move, the first thing his eyes fall on is his half-full bottle of pills on the bedside table. It's a reminder of how difficult of a time he had falling asleep the night before and the night before that. And before that.

Marshall rolls over and blinks at the ceiling. The room is still dark, pre-dawn, not even a tiny hint of sunlight coming through the blinds. The red glow of his alarm clock (5:10) barely illuminates the popcorn above. He closes his eyes again; the warm pressure of blankets is such a tempting nest, pulling him down, drawing him in, farther away from the cold, empty bathroom. His chest feels heavy. His eyes feel heavy. He has gotten a full night's sleep but his face feels too weighted and tired to move.

It doesn't matter how late he goes to bed, Marshall can't help but wake early. It doesn't matter what he does. His room could be a cave, dark as midnight twenty-four hours a day. Silent as a black hole. It wouldn't matter. It's what happens when you're eighty-six years old. It's a cruel joke. Now that he is spending more time awake, he's more alone than at any other point in his life.

He lets his eyes fall shut again. There is so little waiting for him once he gets up. He has hours still before his granddaughter will be there. He wishes, as he does every morning, that he could just sleep a bit later. An hour, even. Anything to fill the time. Remember back when he had to set his alarm for work and actually used the snooze button? Ha!

Sometimes he lets himself stay in bed longer, lolling late into the morning even though he's not sleeping. He keeps a book on his nightstand for those mornings, but right now he's having a hard time focusing on text.

It doesn't matter when he finally decides to get out of bed. No one is holding breakfast for him. No one is excited to start the day. No one to spend the next ten hours with.

Sure, his kids and his grandkids, who now bring his great-grandkids, all visit when they can, taking him shopping when he gets holes in his slacks or bringing him a frozen lasagna when they buy too much. They always send Christmas cards or coordinate with each other to make sure he has a ride to every holiday gathering. But once he's irrevocably gone they will barely notice. They are a team of babysitters just passing him from one caretaker to another.

Like this afternoon. But regardless of how he gets there, Marshall looks forward to this afternoon.

He opens his eyes again, staring into the dark. He sits up in bed, blankets pooling around his waist, his worn white t-shirt hanging off his gaunt angular frame. It's already fairly warm for June, but Marshall is cold all the time. In the summer, he sleeps with four light quilts that he tells himself are just-in-case layers, but each night he ends up using all of them. His thin, knotted hands sort through the blankets, looking for the edges to pull back. Once free, Marshall carefully places his feet on the floor, gearing up his mental strength to bear the weight and joint pain once he stands up.

"Urrggh," he grunts as he gets to his feet, still half bent at the waist. Once he is up and moving around it will get better, but getting out of bed is nearly always the hardest part of his day. Scratch that. Getting out of bed, before dawn in a room that is still pitch black when no one cares whether he does or not is the hardest part of his day.

Marshall straightens up slowly, and drags his feet through the dark room to the bathroom.

8:26am Leah

LEAH HAD WOKEN up at dawn, a couple minutes before her alarm as usual. She had eaten her egg whites with broccoli cooked in coconut oil, had taken a quick jog around the neighborhood and had sat for fifteen minutes of focused meditation all while her family slept. As usual. She has been working on her prosperity affirmations for the last month, so spent five minutes journaling about her money blocks. Her business will hit its next income goal in ninety days or fewer.

Now she is showered and dressed in one of the five identical charcoal gray pantsuits she always wears for weddings, well before she needs to leave for the day. Her dark blonde hair is pulled back into a tight, low bun to stay out of her way during the busy day ahead. She has gathered everything she will need, packed up and in place near the door of her office, but she goes over everything just one last time, because you never know. Leah does not have a reputation for attention to detail from only checking things once.

She had given herself a fifteen minute cushion, just in case, and she texts her assistant Cindy to confirm she will be available in case of an emergency. Always. Just in case. The same routine every weekend. It's near-constant checking, double checking and triple checking, but how else would she coordinate a wedding?

Some of the horror stories she has heard about other weddings make her shudder. A friend of a friend had hired a novice coordinator when she got married and didn't end up having any silverware for her guests. Even worse: they didn't notice until dinner was being served. Her sister-in-law heard a story about a wedding where the officiant had to cancel last minute and they had no backup plan. Although, in that case the couple hadn't even hired a coordinator so there was no one to fix it either. Nothing like that has ever — or will ever — happened at one of Leah Holder's weddings.

She has just finished confirming she has all her vendor phone numbers and back-up contacts when her husband Joe sticks his head into her home office. Their teenage son Dylan is still sleeping in the next room, so he whispers. "Here," he says, handing her a travel mug full of coffee. "In case you don't have time to stop on your way there."

"Thank you." She smiles at him as she takes it, but of course she has time. It's on her pre-planned, printed out timeline — leave twelve minutes early for drive-thru Starbucks, including texting the bride to see if she would like one. Very few of Leah's clients take her up on the offer, but she makes it every wedding day just the same. But still, she thanks him. It *is* thoughtful.

Leah takes a sip of coffee, turns away from Joe and is quickly immersed in her checklist again. Her desk is completely cleared off, save the computer and her meticulously scheduled planner, open to the following Monday morning. Her white board on the wall near the door is completely full with a list of the names and dates for the weddings she has booked the rest of the year. Color-coded by stage in the decision-making *and* payments-received processes. Admittedly, it's a bit complicated — Cindy is still learning the specifics — but it's thorough.

In her hands, Leah holds a yellow legal pad with each and

every action step she is to complete over the course of the day — the first three are already checked off.

"Can we talk real quick? D'you have a minute?" Joe asks her, his voice low.

"Um, yes," she says, slightly distracted. Leah flips to a later page in her legal pad to review her list of bridesmaid names once more before she leaves for the day. "Just a reminder, dear. Today is Ryan and Lindsay's backyard wedding in the Valley. Pertinent contact information and when you can expect me home is already on the fridge just in case. Do you have something fun planned for today?"

He closes the door behind him. She is startled and pulled out of her work. There has never been any reason to close her office door before. Never. It is a point of pride for her that she runs a (more than) full-time business and is still available to her family (most of the time). There is no other chair in the room, so Joe stands awkwardly in front of the closed door.

"I, uh … Yeah. I do have plans today." He scratches his neck and looks around the room, at anything but her. "Not particularly fun, though. Um … Oh, shit." He holds his head in his hands, fingers laced through his salt-and-pepper hair.

Leah blinks at him, trying to understand. Her stomach drops. What on earth could be the problem? Joe never curses. He is usually so calm and prepared. So stable. "Joe, what is it? Are you okay?"

He takes a deep breath and finally looks her in the eye. "I'm going to move out."

She barely hears the words. She can only see his tears. Joe is not a crier.

"What?" she whispers. She feels like her chest has collapsed. Her breath leaves her body. She doesn't realize she is crying until she tastes the saltiness on her lips.

"I'm, uh. I'm going to go move in with my sister. Today. It's closest to my work and she's going to let me sleep on the couch until I find my own place. I'll find one with a room for Dylan too but we can talk about those details later. I'll be gone before you get home." It all comes out in a rush. Leah hears a steeliness enter his tone. He rubs his fists into his eyes, but the tears still flow.

Leah stares.

She doesn't have time for this. What is he thinking? What is he doing to her? Why could he not have waited a day until she has time to talk it over with him? They could work this out — whatever it is — together.

Her eyes are drawn to the whiteboard full of her clients' names and dates looming behind him.

She needs to get herself together. She has a commitment to her job and her bridal couple today. She will have to deal with Joe later. This is not the time. She can fix it tomorrow.

She clears her throat, closes her eyes and takes a couple deep, meditative breaths to calm herself. She gives herself just a moment to roll her shoulders back and sit up a little straighter. "Please. Don't go. Please wait. I don't want you to just run away while I'm gone. Please, Joe. Just … stay one day and we can talk about it."

"No, Leah. I can't." He sounds so tired, leaning, slumped with his back against the door. "It is never just talking with you. Leah, you suffocate me. We've talked about this and it never changes. You always have to fix it and I am so tired of trying to fix it."

"Well, of course I try to fix it," she snaps at him. "You think I should just leave things broken and problems unsolved?" Exasperated, she turns away from him to finish gathering up her notes and organizing them for the rest of the day. What a ridiculous conversation. It's as if he does not know her at all. She can not deal with this right now. She has other responsibilities to take care of.

"No, I know. You're a problem solver. I know. And you're great at your job. It's just … Forget it. I'll be gone when you get home and then I'll call you later in the week. We can talk about it then."

Leah grasps on that last. He'll call her. She still has a chance. She can retreat for now and handle the wedding as she has committed to more than a year ago. He would call her later.

"Alright, then." She nods briskly, all business now that decisions have been made. "We'll talk later. I look forward to discussing this further. Dylan is working tonight but we will both be home by eleven at the latest. There is really no need for you to move out. I'm sure we can fix whatever problem you think we have."

Joe attempts a smile; Leah dabs at the corner of her eye with a tissue. For once she wishes she owned water-proof mascara — there has never before been a need.

"Excuse me," she says as she pushes through the doorway past him. "I need to check my make-up before I leave."

He backs out of her office quietly, not stopping her rush to the bedroom.

8:32am Kristy

KRISTY PUSHES the omelette around her plate. Using her fork, she picks some of the egg off of the piece of bell pepper. Her stomach can handle the soft, cooked vegetable. But not egg. Not right now.

"You want something else, babe?" Her husband Nick stands in the kitchen by the stove wearing her blue checkered apron, the one with the cartoon pig face on it. He's got her UCLA coffee mug in one hand, and a cheap plastic spatula in the other while he makes his own breakfast. "Toast? Yogurt?"

She smiles at him and shakes her head before turning her attention to her food again. Maybe a small sip of coffee would help.

The clock on the microwave behind Nick shines a bright 8:32am. Like an alarm. A countdown. A siren, warning her how few minutes she has left to herself. How little time left to relax, to eat, or to stay off her feet before she's tasked with hunting down someone's cousin from the bar, or waiting silently for the bride's uncle to get out of her way. Just a few hours until she is on her feet, on call, for twelve hours straight.

If her stomach doesn't calm down, Kristy is not going to be able to eat anything before she leaves. Lord, she hopes it's not another afternoon of forcing down almonds and granola bars. You would think after five years of photographing weddings, she wouldn't be so anxious.

8:47am Sophie

SOPHIE WAKES up a little bit before nine. Her blankets have been kicked to the foot of the bed and her nightgown is twisted around her. She carefully untangles herself and strains to listen. She needs to know what to expect before getting out of bed. Is anyone out there in the living room? She has to be really quiet. Because sometimes she goes to bed when her mom is on the phone, and then wakes up with a stranger sleeping on the couch. Once it was two strangers. Sophie has gotten really good at figuring out what's going on in her house just by listening from her bedroom.

Her mom had definitely been talking a lot last night before Sophie put herself to bed. Chatting on the phone and laughing and watching *Grease* really loudly. Sophie had counted — it had been an eight-bottle night before she fell asleep. All of *Grease* and part of *Saturday Night Fever*. Sophie had fallen asleep to the sound of each new beer bottle clinking against and knocking over empty ones. So noisy. On nights like that, she pulls a pillow and blanket over her head. It gets pretty hot under there, but otherwise she would have never been able to sleep.

And she definitely wanted to sleep last night to make this

day come more quickly. Just like Christmas. Today she gets to put on her flower girl dress — the day she has been waiting months for.

Fortunately, this morning, the apartment is silent. No one had stayed the night. Mom must be sleeping still. She would probably sleep for a while longer.

Sophie climbs out of bed and pads down the hallway to listen a little more carefully at her mom's bedroom door. She hears light snoring. Cool. Sophie tip-toes past the door, out to the living room and tries to decide how to spend her morning until it's time to leave. Today is Saturday so she doesn't have to worry about school. It's not one of her dad's weekends. All she has to do is be a flower girl in her cousin Ryan's wedding, but that won't be until later so she can put off waking up Mom.

She guesses she could probably watch most of *Home Alone 2* before Mom wakes up. Even though it's really old, that movie is her favorite. It's a Christmas movie and Dad says it's terrible, but Sophie likes to imagine what she would do if she could go anywhere she wants, without rules or worrying about her mom. Mom has promised they will go to New York together soon. Maybe even next summer, when Sophie is nine.

Hopefully Mom will wake up by herself. Sophie doesn't know what time they have to leave to go pick up great-grandpa Marshall, but it would be better to be late than to wake up Mom. He would understand. Mom wouldn't.

Sophie is hungry. Still quiet on bare feet, she very carefully picks up a dining room chair and carries it over to the kitchen. A year ago, she had to drag the chair but now that she is a much bigger girl of eight years old she can carry it. Once she's up on the chair, she can reach the cereal bowls and cups from the upper cabinets. Then she can carry the chair back to the table, get the Fruit Loops out of the pantry, get the milk and orange juice out of the fridge, and carry all of it over to the dining room table. It takes three trips, but she can make her breakfast all by herself.

She needs to have enough energy for her big day as a flower girl. The fruit in Fruit Loops is probably really healthy. She opens the cereal and fills her bowl, all the way to the brim. The milk is harder to pour. It's almost a full jug and she has a hard time holding the heavy container steady. Her arm trembles under the weight and some milk is poured out onto the table before she is able to guide it over to her bowl of cereal. The milk drips off of the table on to Sophie's feet. She pulls off her wet socks and sets them next to her on the table.

When she was much littler, she would have had to choose between waking Mom up or just staying hungry until she got up. Sometimes — but not often — there is fruit or cheese or something in the fridge, but Sophie likes her bowl of cereal better.

When she goes back to the kitchen to get a paper towel to clean up her spilled milk, Sophie takes a closer look at the kitchen. She had missed it earlier in her focus on not spilling any of her own breakfast, but evidently her mom had attempted some complicated Italian recipe the night before, gave up partway through, and left everything out. Sophie can clean up some of it, but she doesn't really know what is worth saving and what is a complete loss.

She sighs, wishing it were one of her dad's weekends. Her dad and stepmom never left a third of a jar of spaghetti sauce out overnight, with another third of the jar spilled half on the counter, half in the sink.

Kevin McCallister will have to wait. When she is done eating, Sophie carries the dining room chair back over to the kitchen so she can reach the counter. She can at least make sure all the dishes are in the sink and the countertop itself gets wiped up.

Then, maybe, her mom will miss the rest of the mess and not get mad. Sophie misses when she was really little and her mom was more like a mom was supposed to be. She only has three of those memories; she had been four when her parents divorced. But one of them was of helping her mom mix up pancakes. Mom cracked the eggs, and tied a little apron onto Sophie. Sophie had had a special counter-height footstool and was big enough to stir the big bowl all by herself.

She starts wiping the counter and accidentally gets tomato sauce on her nightgown. Sophie wonders where that apron has gone.

9:00am Leah

LEAH WALKS up the long driveway of 18453 Pendleton Lane, coffee in hand. The mid-century, enormous home sits on a flag lot, set far back from the street by a long, shaded pea-gravel driveway. This whole neighborhood south of Ventura Boulevard is full of houses like this — built in the 1960s by fancy entertainment executives with money to spend and room to spread out. These homes have only just started going back on the market in the last ten years; most had been kept in the family since they were built. 18453 Pendleton Lane is the bride's grandfather's house, a two-story Spanish-style with faded terra-cotta roof tiles, a giant, dark oak front door, and bright fuchsia bougainvillea creeping up the white-washed side.

Leah has already been here several times in the months leading up to this day, helping the bride Lindsay and her mother get everything perfect for the wedding today. As she walks up the driveway this morning, she has to remind herself of the details. She's grateful that in her hyper-organization she has everything written down in the white binder in her tote bag, because her mind is not on the house, or on the wedding preparations. Leah cannot stop thinking about what Joe had said to her.

She stumbles, her ankle bending hard. She regains her balance just before falling to her knees altogether. Her coffee is jostled enough to spill over her hand and down her pant leg, dripping into her shoe. It is as if her right foot had decided to go a totally different direction than her left. Her shoe heel isn't broken, thank goodness, but her ankle might be a little sore. She looks at the ground, but can't identify any pebble or uneven edge or anything that would have caused her misstep.

"Shoot," she says. She switches the mug to her other hand so she can shake off the last drips of coffee. The sugar Joe had put in it will now make everything sticky.

She looks down at her slacks — the dark gray will hide most of the stain, but she still should get to a sink. She should try to dab off any of it. *Shoot*, she thinks. *I don't have time for this.* Any cushion of time she has built into her schedule is for cleaning up other people's messes, not her own.

Joe has put her completely off her objective.

But she's putting it all out of her mind. Focus is needed on a wedding day. Particularly a wedding in the backyard of a private home, with so many separate companies to sort out. She will be the point person for every single vendor and question and crisis that arises and she has to be fully present all day. She has to be hyper-aware. She needs to have all the details in her head to be ready for split second decisions if necessary. There will not be any time to think about her husband. So she should just forget him for today. Just for the day.

She walks faster toward the house so she can wash her hand and rinse off the layer of stickiness.

Back at home and once she had gotten into her car, she allowed herself the twenty minute drive alone to think about him. Why was he doing this to her? Hadn't she always done everything for him? She ran through all the reasons that Joe might be thinking about leaving. Simple logic — that's what was needed in a situation like this. Reasoning, evaluating each possibility, and then taking the needed steps to eliminate obstacles. As long as she didn't let her feelings get in the way, she could solve this problem just as she had solved every other.

Is there another woman? Maybe he is in some kind of legal trouble, and is generously distancing himself to protect Dylan and her. Maybe he has heard something about her that's obviously untrue, but he believes it and it repulses him enough to leave. Maybe …

She stops short in the middle of the driveway, almost at the front door. Leah remembers that Joe had specified he would call her 'later in the week.' That's too much time. So much could happen in those three or five days. Maybe she should break her usual 'no personal business on a wedding day' rule just this once?

Leah's thoughts wander so far while she travels to Lindsay's grandfather's house, she only comes out of her fog when she notices she's standing in front of the door, a large iron bird-shaped door knocker at eye level. Today is about Ryan and Lindsay. It is going to be a long day if she lets herself think about Joe and about what could be happening to her marriage.

Leah checks the time — 8:58am — and triple-checks that her phone is on silent (no texts from Joe) before she rings the doorbell, ready to start her long work day.

10:09am Dylan

DYLAN WANDERS out of his room, yawning, rubbing his eyes on the way to the bathroom. His mom has probably already left for the day. What's Dad doing? Is he in the garage? Sounds like someone's stacking stuff. Weird.

He checks his phone — just after ten a.m., so he still has more than five hours before he has to leave for work.

"Dad?" he calls out toward the living room. "Dad?"

When he passes by his parents' room the door is open — not unusual. But the entire surface of their bed is covered with clothes, mostly folded and piled all over.

After peeing, washing his face and congratulating himself for not going back to bed, Dylan wanders around through the kitchen, into the living room. By now it's clear the sound *is* coming from the garage. He walks through the den, his eyes drawn to the partially emptied bookshelves, through the garage door and sees his dad loading what looks like boxes of printer paper into the back of his little Acura.

"Dad, hey." He stifles a yawn. "Uh ... What're you doing?"

"Dylan! You're up! Want to go get some breakfast?"

Dylan narrows his eyes, looking around the garage. "Um …"

His mother has always kept this space meticulously organized, so both cars can fit parked side by side. The back wall of the garage holds tall, straight shelves full of boxes labeled Christmas, Halloween, Painting Supplies and more. Not one of them has been moved or disturbed in any way. What had he heard?

The big door is open so there is plenty of light for Dylan to see what his dad has been doing out here … definitely a stack of boxes. The trunk of the car is open and only has a few boxes in it, but Dad looks beat, like he has been up all night building a house, or digging a moat or something.

"Sure? Uh … I just gotta change." Should he be worried? Shit. Maybe *he* had done something? His dad had that it's-time-for-a-talk look — disappointed eyes and a shallow smile. "Are you okay?"

Joe nods. "Sure, buddy. I'm okay." He nods his head toward the house. "Go change."

Dylan hurries back to his room, and digs through the piles of clothes on the floor. Where are his jeans? Is he in trouble?

Twenty minutes later they are seated into a tiny little two-person booth at IHOP, squeezed back in the corner near the kitchen. In the middle of a Saturday morning, the hum of conversation surrounded them. Waiters step aside to let each other past, occasionally knocking Dylan's elbow as it hangs off the table.

Dylan waits for his dad to speak. He holds the menu in front of his face, scanning quickly. This time he'll try the New York Cheesecake pancakes — he's working his way through the entire list.

Once their food arrives, his dad clears his throat. Repeatedly.

"So, uh… Well. Son, I have something to tell you."

His suspicions are confirmed. Dylan can not remember his

dad ever calling him 'son' except when he is in trouble. He racks his brain, trying to think of what he could possibly have done. Well, at least, what could he have done that his father has found out about? Maybe he changed his mind about letting Dylan drive to Santa Barbara? Dylan tries to arrange his face in an expression of neutral curiosity. "Oh, um. Really?"

"Yes. Well. ... You see... Let me first say that I love you. Your mother loves you. This has nothing to do with you."

"What?"

"I, um." Throat clears. "Dylan, I'm moving out."

"What?"

"You probably noticed all the boxes in the garage. Those are my things. Clothes and books and stuff. I've got a storage unit and I'm going to go stay with Aunt Justine for awhile. Until I find my own place."

"What?" More information is not helping. He's only getting more confused. He cannot keep up.

"Your mother and I are separating."

"What?"

"Stop saying that!"

Dylan looks down at his pancakes.

"I'm sorry. I'm sorry," his dad continues, reaching over to squeeze Dylan's forearm. "I didn't mean that. This is hard for me and I just — I want you to understand. You're old enough to know how an adult relationship works, right?"

"I guess." Dylan picks at his syrup-drenched pancakes, not meeting his father's eyes.

"Right. Well ... God, I should probably tell your mom about all of this before I tell you."

Dylan looks up. "You haven't told her?" That seems unnecessarily calloused, and not at all like his father.

"Well, no. I mean, I've told her that I will be gone before she gets home tonight but we haven't had a chance to talk about why or what it means."

"What the fuck, Dad?"

"Hey. Language. But, yeah, I know. I know." He runs a hand through his hair, which is now standing up straight. Dylan can see now why his dad looks so tired. He has been beating himself up over the whole situation for a while.

They each take a couple bites, trying to enjoy their breakfast while it's hot but not really tasting it at all. After a few moments of silence, Dylan looks at his dad again.

"What about me?"

"Dylan, of course, I love you. I will definitely find a place that you can come live or stay with me. I mean, I don't know." He sighs. "Like I said, I haven't talked to your mom. But we will make this as easy as possible on you. I still care about your mom and I have great hopes that this whole situation will work out. We both love you very much."

"So … so, what then? Is there someone else?"

"No, no. Nothing like that. It's just … things have been difficult. We've grown apart."

"You don't love her anymore? Why not?" He tries to keep the accusation out of his voice. But, before his dad can answer, Dylan remembers having to break up with Jess last fall. She's nice enough, but he just didn't care about her enough to keep dating her. How are you supposed to tell someone that? He feels bad for his dad who is probably trying to do the right thing.

"It's not as simple as that. And I really should talk to her about it. But, hey, once I do I want to be available to answer any question you have. I know this might be hard or confusing to you."

Dylan nods and takes another bite. His pancakes are cold, but he keeps shoveling in mouthfuls. He doesn't want his dad to think the last meal they have together isn't any good.

He imagines his mom, cool, collected, hard as fucking nails, learning that her husband is leaving her and then going off to work all day anyway. She does that a lot — put her work before her family. Or even, put things like her doctors or even DMV appointments before her family. Dylan knows she has a really intense standard for personal responsibility, but for god's sakes. You can go to the dentist next week.

"How're you boys doing?" Their waitress has appeared, coffee pot in hand.

"Fine. Um. Thanks. Can we get the check, please?" his dad says.

"Sure thing."

Dylan glances at his father, who returns to eating wordlessly, and wonders where this decision has come from. Wonders if maybe his dad has gotten tired of not being a priority.

"I'm sorry, Dad."

"Dylan, hey — it's not your fault at all. Don't even think that."

"I know. I'm just sorry. I know how Mom can be."

10:36am Ian

IAN MCKAY IS STILL in bed. He has been awake maybe twenty minutes or so, scrolling through Facebook. His brain feels tight, and his neck and shoulders ache a bit. He has just the hint of a hangover. Last night wasn't much of a party, by his standards. He gropes the side table for the bottle of water without looking. He is sure he left himself a bottle the night before. But he's not paying close enough attention and knocks the bottle to the floor, where it rolls under the bed.

Damn it, Ian thinks as he leans over the edge of the bed. The corner of the mattress presses into his gut as he stretches his fingers to get a grip on the bottle and roll it back out from under the bed.

Finally. Got it. Any farther and he would have had to get out of bed. Ian sits up just a little and leans back against the pillows. Several big gulps of water help immediately. It's hard to drink so much water when he also has to take a leak, but he isn't quite ready to get up yet. He's just a lowly groomsman. Nobody cares that he's still lying around. Hell, it's not even like he has to do anything other than shower. He has no make-up or hair rituals.

Nobody is waiting just for him. Formal photos depend on others as well. Nobody needs him.

He's been listening to the laughing and joking from the other room. There's a lot of light streaming in between the curtains, which had not been closed properly the night before, and he has the vague impression that it is late in the morning.

Some of the other groomsmen are in the next room. If he listens closely, Ian can pick out at least four distinct voices, including the groom. *Is that … Blake? Or, uh … Ugh, I don't know. Too hard*, he thinks. He closes his eyes and lies back against the headboard, water bottle half empty and held loosely in his hand.

The two-bedroom suite they had checked into fewer than twenty-four-hours earlier is utterly wrecked. Ian only has a sheet covering him; every other blanket has been pulled back and is draped halfway on the floor. It's a king-size bed, but he can not remember sharing it with anyone. The ice bucket has fallen over and is soaking a corner of the carpet under the window with melted ice. And that's just the room Ian is in. He doesn't even want to think about the bathroom.

All I know is I am not cleaning it, Ian thinks. He plans to give Ricky his portion of the room cost, a little extra for tip for the sad bastards who have to clean it up and then forget all about it. Hell, that's why they were staying at a Marriott and not at home, right?

Ian closes his eyes, trying to remember why the pillow smells like… He sniffs again. Scotch? He does not remember drinking Scotch. He can only be thankful he doesn't smell vomit. Not in here, at least. He remembers coming in after midnight with the others already here. He remembers drinking some more. He remembers … *Animal House?*

His soon-to-be brother-in-law Ryan raps the door quickly and peeks in. "Hey buddy. It's almost 10:30. I guess we missed our tee time."

"Dude. Totally worth it." Ian grins, remembering what he

had been doing the night before, eleven hours earlier. He wonders if anyone knows yet. Rumors spread. None of the other guys had said anything about Ian coming in late last night. They were too deep in their poker game.

"Ricky is already at the restaurant. We're just waiting for Stu to come down from his room and then we'll go get some food."

Ian nods, trying to decide if he's ready to get out of bed yet. How badly does he really have to pee? He finishes off the bottle of water.

"So, you might want to get in the shower," Ryan prods.

"Yeah, ok." Ian lies back down and closes his eyes. Ryan sighs quietly and leaves.

If he's being honest, this isn't all that worse than any other Saturday morning. The biggest difference is there are a bunch of guys in the other room waiting for him to get it together. At least they're also waiting for Stu. That guy's probably doing something with his baby. Changing her diaper or feeding her, or taking her shoe shopping. Whatever the hell you do with an eight-month-old.

The party won't start without Ian anyway.

Most of the groomsmen Ian had only met the week before at Ryan's bachelor party. Ian likes his new brother-in-law well enough. He's pretty cool. But this is his first time meeting Ryan's friends and they are so boring. Like, four hundred yawns. Probably because most of them are lawyers. They had all spent so much time in school racking up debt that their priorities are all out of whack. Ian is still shocked that Stu and Ricky had spent most of dinner last Friday talking about mutual funds and index… accounts? Index funds? Literally. What the actual fuck? Who even knows what those things are?

The bachelor party had been in Las Vegas, yes, but everyone except Ian had all been far more interested in watching sports with a beer in hand, than in hanging out at the pool and taking in any of the other sights or clubs of Vegas. Why were they even there? Ian had gone out of his way to meet a bunch of girls at once and bring them up to Ryan's suite on his own. Trying to be a good brother, you know? Provide a little of the entertainment? Help out these guys who clearly were not going to get any girls on their own? But while the other guys were polite enough to the girls, not one of them hooked up.

In fact, Ryan even seemed a little mad.

Whatever. He must be whipped, Ian had thought.

He didn't bother trying again. Last night after the rehearsal had been awesome, and Ian doesn't have to worry about the other guys. They all brought their wives. And probably wanted to go to bed at ten-o'clock. Assholes.

Ian has not been to a wedding since he was very little, and he doesn't remember much about it. But, it can't be that different from the movies. Hot girls in tiny, colorful dresses, falling over themselves to talk to the handsome groomsman? After all, one of the bridesmaids already has.

And! Lindsay told him it was an open bar.

Tonight is going to be the shit. Ian grins. He bounces out of bed at this last thought. Shower, then food, then ready to get this party started.

10:49am Amber

WHAT WAS I THINKING, Amber berates herself.

She stands in the shower of her hotel room, two floors above where the boys are staying. She has already been in here nearly twenty minutes, but she continues to let the hot water beat down on her head and back. She clenches and unclenches her fists as her arms hang at her sides, as if she is letting go of the anger and frustration with every flex. She usually keeps a stress ball at work but that doesn't help her here. Her eyes are closed against the plain beige and mauve of the hotel decor. Depressing. But the water pressure is similar enough that Amber can imagine she's home and could just crawl right back into bed. The more she thinks about her mistake of the previous night, the harder she wants to scrub her skin. She may never get clean.

Not that hooking up with Ian had been all that bad. Just stupid. *Stupid. God, Amber, you are so stupid.*

The longer she stays in the shower, the longer she can keep from talking to anyone about the night before. Especially Lindsay. What would she say?

There's a knock on the door, though it is clear whoever it is is coming in anyway. Bidden or not.

"How's my maid of honor?" Lindsay calls.

"Great," says Amber, displaying an enthusiasm she does not feel. "How's the bride to be?"

"Great! Hungry. You gonna be ready soon? It's almost eleven, so if you hurry we should have time for a quick bite before our nail appointment."

"Alright. I'm just about done." Amber turns off the water. A low whine sounds in the wall behind the shower head, the water pressure slowing down. She has been done for at least five or ten minutes already, but hiding in the hot water and steam is far preferable to acting the part of not-a-care-in-the-world maid of honor. She reaches through the gap in the shower curtain, and Lindsay hands her a towel while she continues talking.

"So, I've already heard from the coordinator and everything is right on schedule," she says. "If you get ready fast enough, we can eat, go to our nail appointment, and then get to Grandpa's by one to start doing hair and make-up, right when the photographer arrives. So we should be on schedule. Do you think you can get ready in time?"

"Yes, Lindsay." Amber tries to keep the edge out of her voice. "But not with you in here."

"Oh! Yes! Of course." She giggles. "Oh! One more thing in case I forget later! If you post any pictures can you use hashtag Rowe Wedding? Please? Spread the word? Ok, that's all. Really. Sorry. I'm leaving. You get ready. Just let me know what you need." She closes the door behind her.

Amber feels a stab of guilt. She should be the one accommodating and offering to help. She should be the one who was ready with time to spare so the bride could relax. Hell, she should have already come up with a hashtag for her. But this is the end of a very long two week period in which every single bit of her free time (and money) has been taken up with wedding events, wedding preparation, or just talking about the wedding. Amber wishes she could be alone for a tiny bit longer.

Amber wraps the towel around her hair and steps out of the

tub. The mirror is all fogged over from her long, scalding shower, but it doesn't matter. Amber can not bring herself to care what she looks like for lunch, and they have hired a professional to beautify her for the wedding itself. She is just going to comb her hair and go, no matter what vision the condensation is hiding.

Which is totally unlike the ridiculous effort that had gone into the night before.

The rehearsal had been held at Lindsay's grandfather's Spanish-style house in the late afternoon. It was gorgeous and light-hearted; Amber found herself genuinely looking forward to practicing the wedding ceremony. But, then the entire wedding party and family went to dinner together. Everyone but her paired off with their dates. Even Erica, the only other single bridesmaid, had brought a date to dinner. Granted, it was her brother who Lindsay had known since they were kids, but still. Amber had been the only girl there alone. And after all that effort she had put into how she looked for the evening.

There was a Mexican restaurant nearby that let them book out the entire back room and kept the margaritas coming. She had two. Maybe three. And they weren't small. Lindsay's youngest brother Ian was already handsome, so she didn't need much help. That wasn't the margaritas.

It had started out innocently enough. She teasing him about getting married next. He complimenting her outfit. She insisting he be her 'date' for the evening. He waiting on her a bit and bringing her another drink. Her best friend's little brother was a kind of shield against otherwise being alone all evening in a room full of happily married — or soon to be married — people. Harmless, she had thought.

And it had been. Harmless. Fun. Comforting, in a way, and almost familiar. Until Ian had offered to drive her back to the hotel. She had had more margaritas than he, and she didn't have her car. And nobody else seemed to notice she was stranded. So it was either pay for a cab or ride with Ian. She remembered trying to help him learn how to drive years ago; this would be a fun little trip down memory lane. Plus, he really was very handsome. Hot, even. Delicious. But she couldn't ever tell Lindsay that.

She had pointed out to him the closest entrance to her hotel room, and he had parked in a dark corner across the parking lot. In that very simple turn in the wrong direction, Amber knew exactly what he was expecting ... and had been surprised to find she didn't even mind. In fact, her heart started beating a little harder. Ian had the look of a guy who knew how to kiss. And lord knows she needed to be kissed.

As long as Lindsay didn't find out, being in Ian's arms might make her feel better. About still being single. About spending all her money on a bridesmaid dress. About still being in a boring job when her friends were all starting their grown-up careers. Having fun with Ian would remind her of all the best parts of her life.

Amber sighs, toweling her hair dry. And it had been fun. She wouldn't deny it. She was young and carefree and this hot guy wanted her. But now, the next morning, she sees it had also been stupid. Ian had been nothing but a fling. Now more sober and realistic, she remembers that she can't even have a conversation with him unless she has had a few drinks.

Amber wonders how this evening will go. If Ian will pursue hooking up with her again, or if there will be some other girl to grab his attention. *Let there be another girl*, she prays. He has never been especially focused or single-minded. Amber thinks she can probably avoid him.

She finishes combing her hair and buttons up her blouse. As ready as she would ever be.

11:12am Kristy

QUARTER AFTER ELEVEN. Kristy has about an hour before she has to leave. An hour full of anxiety. The space behind her right eyebrow is throbbing — a stress headache already in full swing. Bizarrely, the tip of her nose always gets a little tingly when she's anxious. It's like a hand that has fallen asleep, but by now she is used to it.

"Are you sure you are still enjoying this?" Nick has asked before each of her previous six weddings. "It's okay if you want to quit. We can make it work."

This is now her fourth wedding in three weeks and she is exhausted. Physically exhausted. Mentally exhausted. Thank goodness she does not have a wedding tomorrow and can maybe take a day off. Although, Lord knows the brides will all be wanting their photos ASAP so she really should spend as much time as she can culling and editing them all.

Yesterday when she was packing all her gear, for the first time in the five years she has been doing this, Kristy thought that maybe, possibly, wedding photography was not the best career for her. It had felt blasphemous to even think. She had taken photos for fun since she was fifteen. And now she was being paid to take photos and eat cake and hang out with people who wanted her to be there on the happiest day of their lives, right? What could be better?

But now all she can think about is how stressed and anxious she is. How will she be able to have this career long-term? How can she make herself sick week after week. She has always loved weddings and loved photography, but somehow the combination of the two always flings her into such stomach-churning anxiety she stays close to the bath-room for the last twenty minutes before she has to leave the house.

But it's not just weddings. Any time she has to take photographs for a client she got nervous. Even though she knows exactly what she's doing, the pressure and expectation and the feeling of being judged pervades all her interactions with clients. Each wedding day is full of uncles who have the same camera as she does or suburban moms who have taken an online class and have at least heard of an f-stop. It feels like every single person watching Kristy do her job is telling them-selves they could do it better.

When she mentions this to Nick, he tries to reassure her. She knows she's being ridiculous. He has tried to show her she's being ridiculous. She has told herself such fears are ridiculous. It doesn't matter. The thirty-six hours before she arrives at any wedding are anxiety-ridden.

So, instead, she has just stopped mentioning it. About a year and a half into photographing weddings full-time she had just accepted this stress as a part of the job. She stocks up on Excedrin, trains herself to work through the nausea, and always packs plenty of snacks since she never eats much during the day before the wedding.

I wasn't even this nervous at my own wedding, she thinks, kneeling in her home office to rearrange her packed bag of equipment.

Nick slouches against the doorframe, coffee in one hand, her water bottles in the other. "Where's the wedding today?" He hands her two water bottles so she can make room for them in the bag.

"Oh, some fancy house in that neighborhood south of Ventura Boulevard. Backyard wedding. I should be home by eleven at the latest."

"And no wedding tomorrow, right? What do you want to do? Should we go out somewhere? You want to stay home? I could grill and make iced coffee and you could spend all day in your bikini by the pool?"

Kristy grins. Her husband is never subtle. He's the best. She is certainly not going to do any work tomorrow, even if she has multiple brides clamoring for their photos.

"We'll see," she replies. "I'll be tired. What do you have planned for today?"

"Nothin'. Not a thing. I might read that new thriller I got, but it's more likely I'll just nap." He laughs at himself. Kristy can already picture the sunburn he'll get from falling asleep near the pool.

"Sunscreen," she admonishes as she finishes organizing each small section of the bag. Each lens needs to be in its place. She will need to be able to make changes quickly, so as to not lose a single second of once-in-a-lifetime moments that she could never ever get back. God. No wonder she was anxious.

Everything fits in one over-the-shoulder camera bag. But it's a very big camera, eight or nine pounds with the lens on. And then, of course, all the extra lenses as well. And the back up camera. Extra batteries, extra memory. External flash. Kristy will have a bruise on her shoulder by the end of the night, just from carrying all that weight around.

She stands up, but before she can hoist the bag to her shoulder, Nick grabs her around her waist and pulls her close.

"You'll be the prettiest one there today, you know."

Kristin laughs in spite of herself. "What about the bride?"

"Nope. Nothin' compared to you."

"You're crazy." She kisses him, grateful for his belief in her and his love for her and his craziness. She can not wait to come home to him.

As they break apart, Nick leans down to pick up her camera bag. "I've got this. You'll be carrying it all day."

She sighs, squeezes his hand and leads the way to the car.

11:40am Marshall

MARSHALL SITS IN HIS WORN, leather armchair, leans back his head and closes his eyes. He needs to let himself rest as much as possible this morning He has already been up for almost seven hours, but with Ryan's wedding he could be awake for another twelve or so. And that's assuming Karen brings him home as soon as it's over. Which … Marshall sighs. He would not be able to count on his granddaughter for that.

He has already showered, eaten, gotten dressed and read two chapters of the McCarthy book he's in the middle of. He can't focus, though. He can't make himself be interested in anything else.

Every day is the same, this evening being the rare exception. At least today he has actual plans and people to look forward to seeing. He'll be with family. Most days he spends his time trying to find the magical combination of activities around meals and doctors appointments to fill his empty days. He might play a few games of solitaire, or see what mindless show is on the television. He should find something to occupy his time. Marshall considers going back to bed. He probably can't sleep, but he could lie there in the dark room and close his eyes for the next couple hours until Karen arrives.

Marshall stands up, slowly, carefully leaning on the arm of the couch until he is steady. He would go for a walk. That's the solution. Get out of his head for a little bit.

He carefully locks his apartment door behind him and heads to the elevator at the end of the hall. He takes it to the bottom floor where a small, sterile lobby will let him out on to the grounds of the complex.

"Good morning, Mr. Page," Missy says as she struggles to move a large potted tree out of the corner so she can clean the floor around it.

"Good morning, dear. How did your son do on his exam?"

"Real good, Mr. Page. Thanks for asking." She beams at him. Missy is here every Saturday, vacuuming the carpets and dusting the light fixtures in the common area of his building.

"Can I help you with that?"

"Oh, no. Thank you." She waves him away as she straightens up. "I'm just fine. You have a big Saturday planned?"

"Yes, I do. My grandson is getting married this evening."

She grins widely. "How wonderful! You must be so proud."

"I am … I am. Yes. Very proud."

"Well, that sounds just lovely." She hurries to get ahead of him so she can open the door. "You have a good day, now."

"Thank you."

Missy would not ever rush him away deliberately, he thinks. But she is working. She must have a lot to do.

The senior apartment complex where his kids have moved him is on a big enough campus to give him a half-mile walk all the way around. Late Saturday morning like this the staff is minimal, but each one of them greets Marshall as he makes his slow circle around the three four-story apartment buildings that form a horseshoe.

Before he had moved into this old person's community, Marshall had plenty to keep him occupied and fill his days. Sometimes he would spend all morning in his garden, and then afternoon fixing a leaky faucet. He had even gotten pretty good using YouTube to learn how to do more advanced plumbing. But since his wife had died, and his kids gently prompted him to sell the house and move to this empty, colorless place where he had no yard and everything was done for him … he could not bring himself to be interested in anything.

Each year is worse.

"Good morning, Mr. Page!"

Marshall slowly walks down the narrow cement walkway that runs the length of his building. Just ahead, one of the gardening crew waves hello with his green glove from where he is kneeling by the flower bed. Marshall recognizes him, though his face and dark hair are shaded by a wide straw hat.

"Good morning, Edgar. Beautiful day for some weeding."

Edgar laughs. "No rest for the wicked, Señor Page."

"Can I help you at all? You know, there's a trick to getting all the roots out when you pull them up. And I mean *all* the roots. My wife and I used to have quite the garden back when we had our house. I spent many Saturdays kneeling in the grass just like you're doing now."

"Oh, no. Thank you, Señor. That's what they hire me for. So you don't have to kneel in the grass."

"I really don't mind." Marshall takes two steps off the path toward the work.

"No, no." Edgar waves him away. "I just have a little bit more to do. You enjoy your walk, Señor."

"Alright … Have a good day."

Marshall likes that he calls him Señor. The slip into Spanish feels more informal somehow, and less like Edgar is staff. When he first moved here, Marshall had been lonely, sure, but also a little excited about all the books and reading he could catch up on since there is no lawn for him to mow. He could finally relax. He had been looking forward to all the money he would save not having to fix his own appliances.

Instead, he felt 'caught up' in only eight or nine months. Now he regularly finds himself bored out of his mind, even after so long being away from the home that he had lived forty-six years with Carol. He has had to get rid of more than half of his things, and the pieces that are left don't fit right in the new space. Nothing feels like it belongs. For eleven years he has lived in an apartment that has felt temporary.

Marshall's wife Carol died twelve years earlier. Cancer. Of course. Seems like it's always cancer. It's taking all his friends. Since then he has kept on going only because he has to. For his kids. He loves his kids — two girls and two boys. They're his whole life now. But Michael died a couple years ago, Susan got divorced and they all lost touch with her.

Carol would have loved today, he thought. When each of their kids had gotten married — even the boys — she had thrown herself in whole-heartedly. When Susan got married, Carol spent the entire spring season leading up to the July wedding personally planting, growing, and caring for roughly fifteen dozen daisies for the reception's centerpieces. Marshall had hinted that it would have been less expensive to buy them, but Carol wanted to be involved. It was her way of showing love. She met with caterers or put together centerpieces or even hemmed bridesmaid dresses. She had been an amazing mother and Marshall missed her more every day.

He has made the full walk around the courtyard. There was just forty feet or so left to his building's door.

The whole family structure had fallen apart without Carol. Marshall can not remember why he keeps making an effort day after day. Books are nothing compared to conversation. A walk around the apartment complex is nothing compared to traveling with her. All the vibrancy had gone out of his life when she died.

Today is different. Ryan is getting married. But tomorrow will be a return of the same.

11:42am Leah

LEAH STANDS IN THE SHADE, checking her phone surreptitiously. 11:42am. Right on schedule.

She shades her eyes against the sunlight. The backyard is bright this early in the day, but beautiful. Once the sun is a little lower, later in the afternoon, it will be breath-taking. Cypress trees line the back wall, a row of sentries protecting guests from the sun and curious neighbors. In a few hours, the sun will move to the far side and cast shade over the partygoers. The whole space is green and lush this time of year. A little hot, maybe, but by the time guests arrive the evening will have cooled pleasantly. June in Los Angeles? Incomparable Southern California? Ryan and Lindsay chose the perfect day for a wedding.

The table and chair delivery is almost all unloaded. Fourteen large round tables have been placed throughout the backyard, strategically allowing both a clear path to the dance floor and a clear line of sight to the head table. Chairs are just beginning to be set up, eight spaced equally around each table. Other members of her day-of team are at work laying out the tablecloths and a third group following shortly behind with the centerpieces. Team work.

Leah glances at her checklist, even though she has already memorized it. Basic set-up by noon. Let them all have a break for lunch, and then make-up artist, photographer, florist and cake will all be arriving within a short time frame. She's ready. Her weddings never veer from the timeline until someone else gets involved. Never.

She stands in the middle of the patio, holding her clipboard and admiring what her team has accomplished. She is confident they can have everything set up by noon as originally planned. She sighs with satisfaction. The wedding will be beautiful. Perfect. Exactly what Lindsay and Ryan have asked for. There is nothing she loves more than seeing the most intricate, layered plans through to fruition. This will be a good day, she'll have two more happy clients, and then she'll go home and crawl into bed —

— And Joe would not be there. Leah stops short. Someone had been walking directly behind her and jostles her as he tries to pass.

She had let herself forget for a few minutes. How could she have forgotten? It all comes back in a flash. Her husband is moving out of the home they share while she is here working. He could be loading his car at that very moment. He isn't interested in talking about it and she has no recourse. She has to remind herself of these things since they had completely left her brain. Has he talked to Dylan? Will she have to explain it to him when she sees him?

How can she go to bed alone tonight? She hasn't been alone in eighteen years.

Leah looks at her phone again. No texts from Joe. *Well,* she thinks. *I suppose it is still early in the day. He probably needs more time to think about what a crazy idea this is. I'll just put it out of my mind and worry about when I get home.*

Where had they gone wrong, she wonders as she meticulously spaces the chairs around the tables that had already been set up. They have been together for so long — why does he have a problem now? Has he really changed that much?

Or has she?

"Leah?" One of her team, Sean, calls from the driveway. "How many extra chairs did you want?"

Chairs? What chairs?

Leah looks around. Oh! Extra chairs for the guests. She does a quick count of tables, a little math and calls back, "A dozen should be plenty."

She must focus. She is grateful Sean is at a distance and has not seen her momentary confusion. She should have had that answer ready. She should have been the one to tell Sean to get chairs before even being asked. This issue with Joe has thrown her completely off.

Darn him, she thinks. Of all the days to drop this on her. He couldn't have brought this up yesterday, when she had been home all day working? Or tomorrow, when she plans to take off work? No, he had to do it today, when she's out of the house all day, busy and almost completely unreachable.

Leah walks the perimeter of the yard. Her eyes are watching her team work but her mind is at home. Where would Joe find the boxes? How much can he pack today? It won't all fit at his sister's. Is he getting a storage unit? Does he plan to take any of the furniture? Has he even thought that far? Why hasn't she thought to ask him that? Maybe she should text him — there are some empty boxes in the garage.

No. Stop it. Leah shakes her head. *Stop trying to fix everything.*

She glances one last time at her phone. No texts. She walks back to the table closest to the house where she has left her tote bag full of emergency things. The phone fits perfectly in an inner pocket, where she can not reach it easily, so she cannot obsess over the lack of communication. She tucks it away, out of sight, out of mind.

Focus is what is needed now.

She can think about all of this later.

11:52am Ian

IAN WANDERS up one of the aisles of Party City. What is it he's supposed to get? *Fuck.*

How the hell Ian got suckered into running this errand he will never know. Somehow in between his shower and checking out of the hotel, it had been impressed upon him the need for someone to go to Party City and the reality that all the other groomsmen had their own responsibilities. Stu had pulled him aside, handed him a fistful of cash and told him four or five things they need to decorate Ryan and Lindsay's going-away vehicle. The other guys all have families to get ready, and Ricky had to go get the table for lunch. There was no one else to do this all-important task.

So now Ian is wandering up yet another aisle, absently looking at the rainbow of paper plates, napkins, cups, plastic silverware, matching tablecloths, streamers and literally more party supplies than would ever have occurred to him to exist. Racking his brain to try to remember what it is he is supposed to buy.

Something to decorate Ryan's car for when they leave the wedding tonight. Ian knows that much.

But that could be anything. ... Probably not these weird lime green plastic butter knives. But this store was crazy. Who could possibly want all this stuff?

"Fuck," Ian says out loud. The middle-aged woman in mom-jeans browsing next to him glares.

The store is enormous and evidently most of the parties in the surrounding area are short plates, or balloons or something else. Saturday late-morning is probably the worst time for Ian to be here. Ricky probably fucking knew that when he made Ian come.

"Can I help you find something?"

Rescue in the form of a teenaged redheaded girl appears next to Ian. The black shirt and shapeless khakis are doing nothing for her figure, but Ian can imagine.

"Hey, thanks ... Felicia," he reads off her name tag. "I don't really know what I'm looking for. What do you recommend?"

She giggles. "For what? I mean, what kind of party are you having?"

"Oh, you know. Just a party. My name is Ian, by the way."

"Nice to meet you, Ian."

Ian flashes his most charming smile at her and forgets why he is there.

12:00pm Amber

AMBER SITS in the next chair over from the bride, her left hand being lotioned and massaged. She watches while the nail technicians fawn over Lindsay. One on each hand, one bringing her a mimosa, one sitting nearby just to talk to her from what Amber can tell. She can't really blame them. Lindsay is petite and pretty and bubbly and blonde and she is wearing one of those cheap white and sequined sashes that says 'Bride,' for goodness sake.

And, of course, this is Lindsay's day. Of all the days, today Amber can not begrudge her the attention. *How many other times in my life have I just watched while people fawned over Lindsay*, she thinks. *I'm used to it. And she deserves it today.*

When they had walked in to Sunshine Nail & Spa — just the two of them, a special little best friends ritual before the wedding — it had taken a full five minutes for someone to notice Amber was standing there and get started with her own manicure after Lindsay had been coddled to. And that only after Lindsay said something to her from the chair.

But even before today, Amber is used to this. It is one of the side effects of being Lindsay's best friend. Worth it, of course.

Lindsay is amazing. Of course. But Amber has had about ten years of living in her shadow. Amber is dark to Lindsay's blonde; she is tall and athletic to Lindsay's delicate petiteness. She is Rizzo to Lindsay's Sandy. Elphaba to her Glinda. Amber's best friend is pretty and popular and smart and always saying the right thing. She even looks a little bit like Kristin Chenoweth, which really isn't fair at all.

Lindsay tells the women surrounding her about the wedding details and her new husband.

"His name is Ryan. He's a lawyer. We've been together two years."

Noisy exclamations echo through the room. Amber has seen this many times before. Women whose husbands are construction workers, retail managers and underpaid teachers are always excited about the prospect of anyone marrying a lawyer and all the opulent fantasies that inspires.

"I'm just not sure about changing my name."

Amber swoops in to do her maid-of-honor duty: shoring up confidence. "Really? I thought you had already decided. Lindsay Rowe is a great name! Mister and Missus Rowe? Ryan and Lindsay Rowe?"

"Really? Better than Lindsay McKay?"

"Not better. Just different. Rowe seems more … professional somehow."

Lindsay looks thoughtful. "You're probably right. Besides, my brothers will both carry on the McKay family name. Well, Blake will at least. I can't imagine Ian ever settling down. Can you?" She laughs, expecting Amber to share the joke.

I should have made out with Blake instead, Amber thinks. *Too bad he has a girlfriend.*

"What happened to you last night? You left dinner kind of early, didn't you?" Lindsay asks.

Amber flushes and bends her head down to look more closely at her nails. "No. No, I don't think so. Most everyone was getting ready to leave when I left."

"Didn't you come in after me?"

"Yeah. I … I went back to the hotel and took a walk."

"In your heels? After margaritas?" Lindsay laughs. Amber flushes again.

"Yes, I, uh … I mostly just walked to the pool, I guess. Stuck my feet in?"

"Huh. Weird I didn't see you since our window overlooks the pool."

"Yeah." She nods. "Weird."

Amber closes her eyes, leaning her head back and willing the whole day to be over. She almost pulls her hand away from the manicurist to chew on her cuticle but stops herself just in time.

The bell over the door tinkles and three girls walk in.

"Stacy! What are you girls doing here?"

Stacy, Gabriela and Brooke, three of Lindsay's bridesmaids, greet the girls with hugs and exclamations. Brooke hands Amber a to-go coffee cup, with a smile.

"Well, we were just next door getting coffee on our way to the hotel." Stacy hands Lindsay a coffee as well. "We recognized your car and thought we would say hi."

"I didn't know you were coming here," Gabriela says. "I just adore this place."

The nail technicians on either side of Lindsay look pleased. "You girls want something done?" asks one of the women. "Wedding party discount?"

"No, no, thank you. We have a couple other wedding errands to run," Gabriela says. Stacy looks meaningfully at Amber behind Gabriela's back, blocked from Lindsay's view.

Amber has no idea what those errands could be. She racks her brain, trying to remember some moment in the last week that anything had been mentioned.

Shit, thinks Amber. *I am a terrible maid of honor.*

12:22pm Sophie

SOPHIE LIES SPRAWLED on the couch, one arm hanging off the side. She finished breakfast long ago and has watched all of *Home Alone 2* and a whole bunch of *My Little Pony*. Too much maybe. Her eyes hurt. Sophie turns off the television and turns to check the clock on the microwave: 12:22. Probably she should start getting ready soon? Her mom always says it took twenty minutes to get anywhere, but Sophie doesn't know if that means twenty minutes to great-grandpa Marshall's and then another twenty minutes to the wedding, or if it means twenty minutes total.

It doesn't matter anyway, because she doesn't know what time they are supposed to be there.

Sophie thinks she might check on her mom, and then she'll get dressed and ready to leave. She doesn't want there to be any delay at all in leaving.

It is supposed to be her weekend with her dad, but because Mom's cousin is getting married and Sophie is in the wedding, they switched. Dad has promised to make it up to her though. Next week she gets to choose between the beach and the zoo.

She loves both, and will spend all of the next seven days trying to decide which one will be better.

This is her first time being a flower girl. The rehearsal last night had been so fun. Mom had been working, so Uncle Tory and Aunt Callie had picked her up after school. They took her to the park, and for a snack ("Don't tell your mom! Ice cream before dinner!") and then they had all gone to the big pretty white house to practice for the wedding.

Sophie is so excited! She is going to be a good flower girl. Aunt Callie has told her all about it. She got to meet her new cousin Lindsay and see her grandparents and carry a silly pretend bouquet made of ribbon. She even got to be the only kid eating with all those grown-ups. There's no 'kids table' when you're the only one.

That's what I'll do, thinks Sophie. *First make sure mom's not awake, just in case. Then get ready. Mom can just zip up my dress right before we leave, but I think I can do everything else.*

Sophie tiptoes down the hall to her mom's room. Very, very slowly she turns the knob so the click of the handle won't be too jarring. It takes forever, but this is the best way. Once she's in, the room itself is brighter than she expected — her mom had left the light in the bathroom on. Mom is turned away from the door, but Sophie knows she is asleep. She is still snoring softly. Sophie steps carefully over some dirty clothes on the floor by the bed, edging her way delicately through the room. There is a yucky sour smell coming from the bathroom, so Sophie doesn't look. She just reaches in a hand and fumbles at turning off the light. Four empty brown bottles on the nightstand. Mom had collapsed on the bed without even changing her clothes.

Once the bathroom light is off, Sophie notices a tiny flash of light near her mom's pillow. It's just a faint little glow that turns on briefly and then off again. The cell phone is announcing that there is only five-percent power left. Quietly, carefully, without waking her, Sophie slips the old iPhone out from under her mom's arm and takes it out to the living room.

She would not like waking up without a phone, but if it is dead then she'll insist on charging it and making them late to the wedding.

Her mom only has one phone charger and she carries it in her purse. Which is probably … Yes. There it is wedged between the cushion and the arm of the couch. Mom always slumps into her spot on the couch when she gets home from work, without even setting down her purse somewhere or taking off her shoes. That's likely where she had been chatting on the phone the night before.

Sophie opens it carefully, just looking for the white cord. Nothing else interests her.

The usual spot to plug in the phone is on the kitchen counter, but Sophie is afraid her mom won't see it there. Should she plug it in back in Mom's room? Or maybe on the floor right where she would walk into the living room? Or maybe the kitchen counter is the best spot after all?

Sophie hates that she always had to be so crafty about every little thing. It feels like lying and Dad says she should always tell the truth. Would this make her mom mad? What about this? Sophie hates to be yelled at, more than anything. And her home is always either silent, or really loud. Sophie would never tell her mother, but she really prefers her dad's house. Where everyone is talking and laughing and her new little brother makes silly, playful noises. And no one yells at each other.

Sophie finally decides the less change the better, and carries the chair back over to the counter so she can reach the plug.

Good thing I cleaned it up in here, she thinks.

12:54pm Kristy

THE MILD, British GPS woman tells her the destination should be on the right, but Kristy is having a hard time making out the house numbers. The mid-day sun casts harsh shadows, essentially obliterating digits here and there. She drives slowly down the tree-lined street, peering at each house in turn.

"Do you see it?" she asks her passenger. "18453? Ugh, I never need my glasses except for times like this."

Marta, the photographer she has hired to help cover the day, squints at the faded numbers on the curb. "I think we passed it."

"Damn it." Kristy turns the car around in a neighbor's driveway and parks on the street. "Well, we know it's around here somewhere. I guess we can just get out and walk."

But she does not get out yet. A quick glance at the dashboard tells her they have six minutes still — 12:54pm. Plenty of time to run through her pre-wedding checklist.

Kristy turns off the car, tightens her mousy blonde ponytail and takes a deep breath. "Ok, let me just go through this once more."

Marta nods. She is a pretty, slightly overweight brunette who has the air of 'what a fun adventure I'm going to have today.'

This is Kristy's first time working with her, but she seems amiable and capable and, thank goodness, has photographed weddings before.

"We have water and snacks, right?" Kristy takes a gulp from her water bottle, even though she knows she should save it. No one ever thinks of the photographers when it comes to the necessities needed to make it all the way through a ten- or twelve-hour wedding day. This might be the only water she has easy access to until she gets home that night. "We synced our cameras, we have two copies of the family shot list, we turned off our phones ... what am I forgetting? How are you with names?"

"Oh, sorry." Marta winces. "Pretty terrible."

Kristy sighs. "That's fine. It'll be fine. The bride and groom are Lindsay and Ryan and everyone else we can figure out as we go."

She rubs her eyes for a few seconds before she remembers she is wearing make-up for once. She is already so tired, but still has a very long, exhausting work day ahead of her. Not only will they be on their feet for more than nine hours straight, but they will have to be charming and personable with total strangers the entire time. All while gently directing them to stand here and corralling drunk groomsmen to move there. On a hot June afternoon.

Kristy checks her eye make-up in the mirror. Not terrible. She licks her finger and rubs and the dark spot under her right eye where she had accidentally smudged her mascara.

"So, we still have a couple minutes. Lemme tell you about the timeline, they don't want to see each other before the ceremony."

"Awww ... traditionalists."

Kristy rolls her eyes. "But, of course, only gave us a tiny window after the ceremony to get all their photos together. All of them. Why don't people listen to me? It might be their first wedding, but it's not mine. I'll just have to talk to the coordinator. Leah Something. See what she can do."

"So, they're doing a cocktail half-hour?"

"Yeah, but let's go back. Ok. Girls are getting ready here. We should have plenty of time for that. Boys are getting ready at a hotel. Again, they didn't listen to me and apparently don't care about getting-ready photos. Although, you know when I send them the photos they'll notice." She sighs. "Anyway, then bride and bridesmaid photos, groom and groomsmen photos, a few family photos at five or so, and then ceremony at quarter 'til six."

"How do you want me to cover the ceremony?"

"Um … I dunno. Wait 'til we see how it's laid out? After the ceremony, thirty minutes for big family photos and the bride and groom photos. Then first dance. Then dinner and we can finally take a break. The reception basically takes care of itself. Until they ask me how to cut the cake, of course."

Marta laughs. "Sounds good! I love weddings."

Kristy tries to remember back to when she had loved weddings.

When she had left, Nick was about to get into the pool. Beer in one hand, book in another, their dog already napping in the shade under the patio table. Nick has no plans for the rest of the afternoon other than to enjoy his day off. How very much she wishes she were home with him. She could almost cry thinking about it.

But, Kristy reminds herself, she's lucky. Not everyone gets to do this. This is a great job. Really. A ton of photographers would kill for her clients and career. She really should not be complaining at all. Right?

"Are you married?"

"Me? No. No, I've been dating this guy for a bit, but not married."

"What would you be doing today if you weren't shooting this wedding?"

Marta looks thoughtful. "I dunno. Maybe just marathoning Netflix? Just like other days. Weekends are no big deal to me." She shrugs.

Kristy makes a fist involuntarily. Well. How nice for Marta.

She reaches down and pops the trunk, exiting the car wordlessly. It had been so difficult that morning to pick an outfit that would work for both working in the hot sun all day and still be appropriate for a wedding. She was wearing a sleeveless black dress, leggings, and black tennis shoes.

"Damn it," Kristy says again. "I forgot to bring a handkerchief."

Marta looks confused. "You're going to cry?"

"No. It's just … the sun hates me and my pale Irish skin. I am going to be so sweaty today any time we are outside and I meant to bring a handkerchief."

"Oh." Marta nods. Clearly, the idea of sweating in the sun is foreign to her.

They heave their camera bags out of the trunk.

"So, how many weddings do you shoot every year?" Marta asks, changing the subject.

"Twenty-five or thirty or so."

"That's great! Busy!"

"Yep. I would love to be one of those photographers that charges a zillion dollars per wedding and only shoot five each year, but, you know." Kristy smiles. It's one of the reasons she started her own business in the first place, so she could control how much she works. But, as always happens when building a business, she had found herself doing more and more of the administrative and businessy things that frustrated her and less and less of the photography work that she loves.

"It must be this way," Marta says, starting to cross the small residential street to the opposite sidewalk.

Kristy can already feel the weight of her camera bag weighing her down. Backup camera, plus five lenses, a big flash, extra batteries, giant water bottle, snacks, sweater in case it gets chilly, business cards, as well as her phone, keys, and ID. Just in case. And nowhere to leave it since thieves have been known to just walk in to weddings and leave with what they want. She has got to carry all of this with her.

Her shoulder is already starting to ache.

Kristy sets her jaw in a smile she doesn't feel, mentally preparing herself for the next nine hours.

"Ready? Here it is," she says, and leads the way up the long driveway.

1:12pm Dylan

DYLAN DRIBBLES. Four times. Pauses, then takes the foul shot. He's on a streak of six in a row so far — not his best, but what can be expected? He can barely focus on the ball in his hands, let alone getting it into the basket.

It's a good thing his Saturday is so free. He couldn't think about anything else. No homework. No plans with friends. He's probably supposed to be mowing the lawn right now, but there isn't any way his dad would make him do that.

Joe steps out onto the front porch to where Dylan is playing in the driveway. Dylan flushes with guilt, sure he is going to be told off for not doing his chores.

"Hey. I'm all packed up."

Dylan stops dribbling. This is it.

"You sure you can't stay till Mom gets home? You can talk about it? I could be there?"

"Dylan. No, I'm sorry. You know how your mom is."

"But, Dad — "

"No. I'm sorry. She is totally overly rational. Any conversation that we have would end in me giving in just because she won't. She doesn't understand compromise. She will never admit she might be wrong."

Dylan closes his eyes. That's true. Dylan learned a long time ago it is always easier to just let her win.

"I have to do it this way. I know this will make me happier in the long run," his dad continues. "We will all be happier. Eventually."

"Fine. Whatever." Dylan resumes his dribbling and turns toward the basket.

"I know, buddy. I'm sorry. I don't know what else I can say." His dad shrugs and returns inside.

Dylan stays quiet. He doesn't know what to say either. He's so angry at both of his parents.

Dylan is not looking forward to work tonight.

1:24pm Ian

IAN MEETS Ryan and Stu in the lobby of P.F. Chang's. He has to push through a young family with two little boys still dressed in their soccer uniforms and cleats. Apparently this is where all the post-sports families come to stuff their faces. Ricky, Ryan's best friend from college and the best man, has chosen the restaurant, is holding their table and ordering appetizers before anyone else arrives. Fair enough. P.F. Chang's seems kind of girly and not what Ian would have picked, but whatever.

Early afternoon on a Saturday, the lunch crowd is already well entrenched. Apparently Ricky had arrived a whole hour earlier to put their name in. Sucker.

The hostess leads them across the restaurant, between full tables of chattering guests, to a large booth in the back room. The room isn't quite empty, but it certainly isn't in the busiest hub of the place. Ian is used to this; he often gets relegated to back corners of restaurants. As if just by looking at him they know to expect him to get rowdy. He chuckles to himself.

Too bad. Ian will take responsibility for the entertainment and keep the party going. They need him. Bunch of dull duds already tied down. Not one of them shows a hint of a hangover and they all seem remarkably chipper for this early in the day.

Most of these guys are already married — Ryan is the last one of all his friends. They aren't Ian's friends anyway. Ryan just asked Blake and him to be in the wedding party because of the brother thing. It's nice of him, and he knows Lindsay was happy about it. But, really? Ian would have been fine being left out.

This is only the third meal Ian has ever had with all these guys. During the bachelor party weekend, Ian went off by himself after the first night. He didn't think Ryan would really mind, since the dude had seemed so uninterested in the girls Ian had hooked him up with. Then, the rehearsal dinner last night, when they all brought their wives. And now this. Ryan's last meal as a single guy.

Whether by coincidence or design, their table has been assigned the hottest waitress in the place. Sure, she's wearing her conservative, buttoned-up uniform, but Ian can just tell she's hot underneath all of that. Bonus: since she's here at lunch, she probably will be off work tonight when the wedding is over.

Ian calls for her attention before she can even open her mouth.

"Hey, yeah. What's your name? Maria?" He looks her up and down, pleased. "Ok, Maria, I need a round of beer to start with. Whatever you think. Pitchers or however you guys do it here. And then you should also know that this guy…" Ian claps his hand on Ryan's shoulder. "This guy is getting married later today, so I want you to do your best to remind him what he is giving up."

Ian laughs loudly and looks around for the guys' reactions, but they only kind of smile politely. He doesn't see Maria's reaction, but he doesn't need to. That is her job, right? To wait on the table and make them all feel cared for. She's probably already looking forward to a big tip from all these guys. Stu looks a bit shocked and gets up to lead her away, talking softly. Maybe ordering more drinks, Ian thinks.

Once he has sat down again, Ian's older brother Blake leans over. "Hey, settle down. This isn't that kind of party," he says softly. The other guys are all talking over him, apparently not paying attention or at least pretending not to. "This is just lunch. Before we all have a long afternoon and evening. Just relax and eat."

Ian just scoffs and leans back in the booth. It's never just lunch. Hadn't Blake noticed that the restaurant had sent them their hottest waitress? This is exactly how final meals should go. Ryan should be thrilled.

He doesn't join in the conversation — Ricky asks about the honeymoon, and Ryan launches into a long, detailed description of all the zip lining, snorkeling and surfing they were going to do in Costa Rica. It makes Ian tired just listening to it. But he listens closely, in case he could find a good opportunity to jump in and change the subject.

Is this what it's like to be married? No longer even interested in admiring the hot piece of ass that we get handed as a waitress? Ian can not imagine ever coming to that point.

But Blake keeps giving him warning looks, so Ian keeps his mouth shut and just watches Maria whenever she comes by.

1:44pm Amber

AMBER SITS QUIETLY STILL, looking down as instructed. She has laced up her fingers and wedged her hands between her thighs so she won't be tempted to bite her nails. Such a mindless habit when she doesn't have anything to do with her hands. It gets even worse when she's anxious like today. The make-up artist, Cristina, applies her delicate brush to Amber's eyelid. So many layers and delicate little touches. Lindsay insists they all wear fake lashes, and the added weight is making Amber just want to close her eyes and go back to bed. She sits near the window in the house's master bedroom. Nowhere near a mirror. But that's fine. Amber is past caring what she looks like today. She trusts the make-up artist to keep her presentable, but other than that what does it really matter?

It's not like she has a boyfriend to impress. Or that there is any prospect of meeting someone at this wedding. Or even that she wants to get Ian's attention again. Weddings are a hard place to be when you're lonely.

Amber will be the first one of the girls ready to be photographed. The other six are having fun laughing and chatting. Which is probably why they aren't even close to being ready. Once Cristina finishes her eyes, Amber just has to put the dress on and do one last check of her hair and make-up. She still has to find her genuine smile though.

There are still four hours before the ceremony and Amber is already exhausted.

Lindsay's kind-of sister-in-law, Blake's girlfriend, Stacy plops onto the edge of the bed next to Amber. She leans close and whispers, "I saw you last night."

Amber does not have the energy for any witty comeback to change the subject.

"What?"

"I saw you. After dinner. In *someone's* car." Stacy raises her eyebrows, trying to look at Amber meaningfully, but really just emphasizing her very large eyes.

"What?" She refuses to make this easy. If Stacy thinks she is on to something she will have to come out with it herself. Amber is admitting to nothing.

Stacy snorts. "Whatever. You don't have to tell me about it. Just to check though, does Lindsay know?"

"Look down," says Cristina.

"Does Lindsay know what?"

"Well, I'm going to assume that means yes so I guess I'll just ask her what she thinks since you don't want to talk about it."

"Wait wait wait." Amber is defeated. But also a little impressed at the way Cristina is pretending not to hear any of it. Professional. "What did you see?"

"I told you. You. In a car. Ian's car. I couldn't really see in, though, since the windows were all fogging up."

Amber groans. "Damn it. I am such an idiot."

"Look up," says Cristina.

"No, wait." Stacy's tone changes immediately from teasing to caring. "Why are you an idiot? Do you like him?"

"Not like that. I just … I'm just an idiot. I had had too many margaritas and he can be so charming."

"Yeah?" She looks at Amber expectantly.

"Yeah." She shrugs.

"Hold still," Cristina says.

"That's it. It was stupid. I just wanted to be kissed. And, really, he is a good kisser. Too bad he also talks with that mouth."

Stacy laughs. "I know exactly what you mean. Youngest child thing, I think."

"I just want to forget the whole thing. Especially before Lindsay finds out. Did anyone else see?"

"Not that I have been able to tell. We'll see. Lindsay would be cool about it, but you're right. Better everyone just forget it."

Amber smiles. Grateful, but still so irritated with her poor decision.

"Are you ok?"

Amber brightens her smile. "Yes, fine. Of course. Good. Last night was just weird. Let's just forget it."

"Ok. Cool. Well. Let me know if you need to talk. Or if you need me to, I don't know. Shoot Ian with a tranquilizer or something."

They both laugh.

"So, what errands did you have to do this afternoon?" Amber asks, her voice low. She doesn't care how obvious it was that she was trying to change the subject.

"Oh!" Stacy moves even closer so she can whisper. As if *this* is the really important secret, not the fact that she had seen the maid of honor making out with the bride's brother the night before. "We just got some supplies to decorate their car. Ricky and Blake and some of the others are going to take care of it."

"Oh, great! Yeah, I think Blake mentioned that to me," Amber lies.

"Right, so then, you know. Balloons and writing on the windows and all."

"Right. Good." Amber nods.

"I'm sorry, can you not nod? I need you to look right at me," says Cristina.

"Sorry," Amber whispers.

"Well, anyway. Let me know," Stacy says, squeezing Amber's shoulder lightly and moving away.

Amber had almost forgotten Cristina is there. And now she's looking directly at this stranger who just heard the one thing she is most embarrassed about.

"Ian is Lindsay's youngest brother," she says.

Cristina nods. She leans close to Amber's face, examining her work so far.

"I was a wreck last night and kind of hooked up with him. It was stupid."

"No need to explain," she answers, finally looking Amber in the eyes. "We all do stupid things."

"I guess."

"You've got to stop talking now because I'm going to do your lips."

"Oh, ok. Sorry."

Amber tries holding perfectly still. What a strange, intimate experience, having someone so close to her face, touching her mouth so gently …

Ian had been so gentle, too. Amber had been surprised at how tender and attentive he was. It did not seem like his personality at all, to pay attention to other people. At least she had enjoyed it at the time.

"Ok, rub your lips together." Cristina demonstrates. "And take this Kleenex to blot gently. Perfect. I think you look lovely, but take this mirror. Let me know if there's anything you want to change."

Amber examines her reflection. Not terrible. It still looks like her, after all. "Good. Thanks." She tries out a smile in the mirror. See? No one will be able to tell it isn't real.

2:02pm Leah

LEAH STANDS close to the house, in the narrow strip of shade, watching her team set up the centerpieces. She is tired of hovering, but until the cake arrives or the florist finishes the ceremony set-up there's not much she can do.

Confident that all is going according to schedule, Leah slips back into the house where she had left her binder of details and purse in the shadowy corner of the dining room. The blinds are still closed and the room is a cave. Lovely, exposed wood beams run the length of the ceiling, but suck all the light out of the room. With the adorable breakfast nook in the next room, the dining room probably has not been used since Thanksgiving.

Leah fishes her cell phone out of the pocket of her tote bag and sets it on the table, directly in front of her. A quick button tap shows her the time — 2:02pm — and nothing else. Not a single text message or missed call. She hits the table with the palm of her hand in disappointment. She has been so good about not texting Joe or checking her phone too obsessively, she feels like she should be rewarded with something. Even just something little. 'I will wait til tomorrow,' or 'I want to talk about this' or maybe even 'I was wrong.' Anything?

She is always very careful not to book two weddings in the same weekend, so she can at least have one day off with her family all together. Now that she really has a moment to think about, she feels more certain that Joe deliberately waited for a day that he knows she would be gone. This isn't an unfortunate coincidence — it's strategic.

As she stares at her phone, a new text comes through. It's from her son Dylan: 'talked 2 dad.'

She stares a moment longer, waiting for the next part of that thought to arrive. Nothing. Is he still typing? Is it a typo? Maybe he is telling her, like a command, to talk to dad, telling her to break her wedding day vow of silence. Maybe he knows something she doesn't. Should she respond? Is Joe trying to get to her through their son, pulling him into some kind of mind game to punish her?

She shakes her head. No, that's not what this is. He would assume she isn't checking messages all day. She never has before; why would today be different?

Leah lets out a long breath and leans forward, forehead resting on the table, eyes closed.

She's going crazy. That's what this is. She's letting this one thing that she doesn't even have control over affect her whole day. She either needs to let it go …. Or text her assistant so Leah can leave the wedding and go home. It tempts her. Leah taps through her contacts to find Cindy's number. Her thumb hovers over the 'call now' button.

The one thing stopping her is the fact that she has never left a wedding in the middle of the day. She sighs. Leah is not willing to break that. She is justifiably proud of that, and she has never been one to let other people's actions manipulate her own. Maybe she'll wait a little longer. Once more setup is done. That will give Joe or Dylan more time to contact her.

There's a knock at the front door. That would be the cake. Leah snaps back into gear — she is running a wedding, after all.

3:14pm Sophie

"SOPHIE!"

Her mom calls from the bedroom. It sounds more like a croak than anything else. Her voice must be tired from talking all night. "Where's my phone?"

"It's charging!" Sophie calls back. She runs over to where the phone sits on the counter. She notices a missed call from her great-grandpa Marshall. Sophie unplugs it — 3:14pm, charged to eighty three percent — and carries it over to her mom's doorway.

"Um, Mom? What time are we supposed to leave?"

"Jesus, Sophie, I don't know. Give me a minute to wake up at least."

"You missed a call from Great-grandpa."

"Shit!" Her mom snatches the phone from her, quickly tapping and swiping.

Sophie watches as her mother has all of a sudden woken up completely to return the call. Raising her voice a little, since he refuses to wear a hearing aid, she says, "Grandpa? It's Karen. Yeah, I'm sorry we're just running late. Sophie is throwing a tantrum. The little brat." She doesn't meet her daughter's eyes.

"Yeah, so we'll leave here as soon as we can. Ok. Yep. I'll see you soon. Love you, too."

She taps her phone to end the call and lies back down, eyes closed.

"I'm not throwing a tantrum," Sophie says, almost at a whisper, so maybe her mom could pretend she doesn't hear it.

"I know, Soph! God, give me a break. Sometimes you just gotta make excuses people will understand. Great-grandpa is old and if I told him that I had just woken up he would have lectured me and taken up more time. Understand?"

Sophie shakes her head. Not really. Dad always says they should tell the truth. But now Mom is saying it was better if they don't. Being a grown-up seems so confusing. Always having to know what to say and what to do and take care of other people. Her mom never seems to enjoy it.

"Baby, can you bring me a beer from the fridge? I just need a little something then I can get up so we can go. You look so pretty in your dress."

"I need you to zip up the back, please."

"After you grab me a beer? Thank you, sweetheart."

Sophie leaves her mom still lying in bed while she goes to the kitchen. There are still six or seven beers in the fridge, luckily. She grabs one and the bottle opener and carries them both back to the bedroom, where her mom sits up in bed with her feet on the floor.

"Thank you, baby. Do you think you could also take these empty bottles to the kitchen for me? Be careful not to let them touch your dress."

Sophie obeys without comment. She guesses that maybe they are already late, so she has to help her mom as much as she can so they could leave so they can pick up Great-grandpa so they can get there before the wedding so she can be a flower girl. She desperately wants to be a flower girl tonight.

It takes her two trips to take all the bottles to the kitchen where the trash can sits overflowing. She would have to remind her mother tomorrow to take that out. Her dress still hangs open behind her. But at least now her mom is up and out of bed, sitting in the living room, drinking her beer, looking through her phone.

"Mom? Could you zip up my dress, please?"

"What? Yeah, c'mere."

Sophie feels her dress close up, tightly around her body and thinks, *ok. I'm finally ready*. She sits in the brown armchair across the living room and watches, patiently, for her mom to get ready to go.

3:21pm Kristy

"AREN'T the guys supposed to be here?" Marta asks.

"Yep." Kristy checks the time. "Have you ever known a wedding to run on time?"

They wait in silence a moment before Marta speaks again. "Lindsay seems so sweet. Do you know how she and Ryan met?"

"Work? I think? They're both lawyers."

Kristy sets her big camera bag at her feet, leaning against her legs while she tries to fan herself with the folded-up shot list. She and Marta stand on the gravel driveway near the house, waiting for the groom and his groomsmen. She has just finished photographing the bride and her bridesmaids, and the girls hustle back inside and up the stairs to stay hidden for the imminent arrival of the groom. Marta has already captured the ceremony site, and the cake but everything else they have to wait for.

This is the frustration of being a wedding photographer — hurry up and wait. Be there and be ready at a second's notice, even if you have to wait hours for the moment because you will never have it again. The moment when the bride and groom see each other for the first time, they'll be surrounded by a crowd of standing people, and somehow Kristy is expected to photograph that 'intimate' moment without being in anybody else's way. The reception set up will be done all of three minutes before they let guests in, and somehow Kristy is expected to get all her photos during that three minutes.

She sighs.

What kind of job could she get that she won't have to deal with people and ridiculous expectations in a high pressure situation? Garbage collector? Data entry? Maybe she could sort packages at the post office. Anything.

But, no. She's here. On her feet for almost three hours with another three or four to go before she can sit. And now, even though they still have so much more to photograph — the boys, the rings, the details, the family, let alone all of the ceremony and reception — they just have to stand around waiting because none of that is done.

Kristy's phone vibrates with a text from her husband. He's sent a photo of their dog swimming. *Ohmygod, swimming sounds fantastic*, she thinks still fanning herself. *I could be swimming right now instead of waiting for a bunch of drunk guys to show up.*

"Lindsay looks just beautiful, don't you think?" Marta says from behind her camera. She scrolls through the photos she has just taken. "That dress? I love shooting weddings that have spent some money."

Kristy smiles. That's true. She has enjoyed photographing weddings so much more now that she has priced herself out of the low-budgets. Thank god for Marta. Her chipperness may be annoying, but she helps Kristy remember why she has always loved weddings.

She often tells Nick she doesn't love photographing weddings, but she loves having created those photographs. There are always two or three stunning photos of the day that almost make the whole ordeal worth it.

Almost.

"How often do you shoot weddings?" she asks Marta.

"Well, let's see… Last year I had ten. This year I have fourteen. Next year I have eleven booked already."

"That's great!"

"Yeah, you know? I really love it. I used to do admin work at a doctor's office and it was just awful. Sick people are mean. But this? Everyone is always so happy to see me. I actually love working seven days a week."

"Hmmm…"

"Oh, I know, I know. I should take days off. And I do. But I always spend those days looking forward to meeting with a new bride and groom."

Kristy smiles. "That's great, Marta. It's so nice that you've found something you love."

An older couple Kristy recognizes as Ryan's parents walk up the driveway, hand-in-hand. They look sweltering in their formal attire — it will be perfect for later this evening, but in the afternoon sun it seems impractical.

"Hello, my dear," Mrs. Rowe says, greeting her with a delicate handshake. "So nice to see you again. This is my husband Jerry. Are we the first ones here?"

"I think so. Lindsay's parents are around somewhere and all the girls are upstairs in the master bedroom if you want to take a peek."

"Let's go inside where it's cool, at any rate," Mr. Rowe says, already leading the way.

Kristy doesn't argue. Without the groom, there's no reason for them to stick around outside waiting. She starts fanning herself again, staring back down the long driveway.

3:34pm Ian

IAN PARKS A FEW HOUSES AWAY. The narrow residential street is already filling up. He's maybe only four minutes late, but it could be more like twenty. No one had given him a straight answer. Oh well. Who the fuck really cared? The wedding doesn't start for at least a couple hours. He has come straight from lunch. Well, not straight. He had stopped to buy a big soda and some condoms. Had to make sure he was fully prepared for the rest of the night.

He checks his pockets one last time: wallet, keys, phone. Sunglasses on his face. He has put one condom in his wallet and another in the ashtray in his car, and the rest of the box is stashed under the passenger's side seat. You never know. Ian hasn't ever been to a wedding as an adult, but he has seen enough movies to know there has to be at least one bridesmaid or guest that drinks just enough to throw herself at a groomsman.

And Ian intends to be there waiting and ready.

Especially since there had already been one bridesmaid who had thrown herself at him.

He gets out of the car and crosses the quiet residential street.

From the foot of the driveway, he can't see more than one or two guys in suits, so at least he knows he's not late.

When he walks up the driveway, he notices there are still a couple of the bridesmaids waiting outside. Have they already finished with their photographs? He's surprised to see them in floor-length black gowns. That's not nearly as much skin as he had been hoping. Lindsay is nowhere to be seen, but Amber and a couple other girls, whose names he doesn't know, are standing in the shade chatting.

The photographer stands not far in front of him. She also wears a black dress — not as long as the bridesmaids', but still not short enough for his taste — and leans forward a little bit to take Amber's portrait. Ian stops behind her to admire the view. Of Amber, too. He checks out the photographer for just a second before turning his attention to Amber. If he plays it right he could very well duplicate the previous night. And more. Amber is pretty enough, but last night she had seemed sad and desperate. The perfect opportunity for Ian.

She doesn't seem to notice him, but he isn't worried.

She will.

3:49pm Sophie

SOPHIE SITS on the floor of the hallway, listening. The toilet flushes. There is some muffled shuffling, with sounds of something soft being dropped on the floor. And then the click, gushing sound of the shower head being turned on.

Now that her mom has finally gotten in the shower, Sophie feels better. Her tummy had been starting to hurt, the longer that Mom just sat, starting her second beer, tapping messages on her phone to people Sophie doesn't know. She hasn't asked her mom about curling her hair or letting her wear make-up. Maybe there will be time for her to ask Aunt Callie when they get to where the wedding will be. Sophie knows that's where Lindsay and the other girls were getting ready so maybe one of them could help her.

Sophie moves down the hall to the living room to wait and pretend to watch more *My Little Pony*. It's the only thing she can really do since she's too worried about being late. But she has seen all these episodes before, so she doesn't have to really pay attention. Instead, her ears zero in on the sounds coming out of her mom's room. The shower water turns off. Sophie hears more soft shuffling. The bathroom door clicking open. And then nothing. No sounds for what feels like forever. Until, finally, Sophie hears rustling in the drawer where her mom keeps the combs, blow dryer, closet door opening and closing, more rustling of clothes. With each sound, Sophie can just picture what her mom is doing, getting closer and closer to leaving time.

"Sophie! Honey, bring me one more beer and then we'll be ready to go."

Sophie hopes that is true. She turns off the TV and carries another cold beer into the bedroom. The bottle opener still rests on the nightstand from the last one. She hands over the drink and settles in to watch her mother. She is so beautiful. Sophie hopes that someday she can be half as pretty as her mom.

"Are we almost ready, Mom? Should I put my shoes on?"

"You don't have your shoes on?" Her mom looks sharply at her while still fastening her earrings. "Yes, go. Get your shoes. I don't want to have to wait for you. We need to go get Great-grandpa."

Sophie finds her special flower girl shoes in a box on her dresser and hears her mom call after her, "And grab a jacket, too, just in case."

Shoes? Jacket? Ok, she's ready.

"Ok, honey? You ready? Shit, we were supposed to leave twenty minutes ago. And we still need to get food. McDonald's OK? Ah well. Fuck it. Where are my keys? God, I hope Siri knows where we're going."

Sophie bounces a little on her toes. This is it! In just a few hours she will get to walk down the aisle with her basket of flowers. Her mom quickly swallows the last bit of her third beer and ushers them out the door.

4:00pm Dylan

DYLAN WALKS up the long gravel driveway to the Spanish-style house where he will be working for the evening. At the beginning of the year, not long after he turned sixteen, his mom had gotten him a job with one of the caterers she worked with. He has already worked at five different weddings that his mom has coordinated. He doesn't want to admit it, but it's kind of cool of her to get him a job somewhere other than directly with her. And he discovered that he's actually a pretty good waiter.

Waiting tables at events is different than at restaurants, he assumes, but he likes it for the most part. Especially weddings. Everyone is so happy to be there at all; there's very little complaining, no one sending back food, or acting entitled. This could be a good job for a few years for him. He actually doesn't mind working.

Tonight is different, though. Dylan doesn't want to see his mom. She has driven away his dad and he's frustrated with her. He almost thought about calling his boss and telling her he's sick from work tonight, but he likes Cheryl well enough to not want to punish her for his mom's actions.

His mom stands in the center of the path in front of the

house, watching the groom get his photo taken. She notices him, and smiles in greeting, but turns her attention immediately back to her client.

She could at least say hi. He walks right up to his mom until he is standing close at her elbow.

"I talked do Dad," he says pointedly.

She looks at him, surprised. "Ok, Dylan. We'll talk about it. But I'm working right now." She looks away, continuing in a hushed voice. "And so are you. Let's stay professional, please."

His mom can be such a cold bitch sometimes.

"Fine. Whatever."

He starts to walk away, but he is just too angry. He can not let her get away with this.

"But, you know what?" he says, turning back around. "He has the right idea. I think he *should* move out. And as soon as he has a place I'm moving too." Dylan keeps his voice as cold and unfeeling as he can. Just like hers. He can't trust himself to say any more without crying or yelling at her, so he walks away.

He wants his mom to call after him. To run after him and hug him and tell him she's sorry and explain everything. He just wants his parents to be parents and fix this. He feels the tears coming now. He doesn't look back.

4:09pm Leah

LEAH WATCHES DYLAN WALK AWAY, back to the driveway behind the house where the caterer's truck is parked. He's already taller than Joe, but still has that sweet teenager awkwardness to his movements. Like a baby bird, that has not yet gotten accustomed to his long limbs and is only barely hanging on to his balance. Leah sees the little boy in his walk, still. But now her son has to grow up too quickly and it breaks her heart.

She tries to fight back tears. "Shoot!" she whispers, gently dabbing the tears from her eyes to try not to smear her makeup. It kills her to have to put her son through this.

It's not your fault, she reminds herself. *Joe is doing this this to our family.*

She stands to one side of the dance floor (or, rather, tiled patio outside the kitchen), in the shade of the house. Holding her hand up to block the sun is the only way she can see what her team is doing. The angle of the sunset is beaming down perfectly in her eyes. The tables, chairs, centerpieces and individual favors are all set up. Everything appears to be done for now.

She's not needed at the moment.

Tomorrow, or as soon as she can after this wedding day was over, Leah will sit Dylan down and explain everything. Well, as much as she can considering she doesn't even know what is really going on. It's a shame they have driven separately. A ride home would have been the perfect opportunity.

Leah checks her phone. No text from Joe, still. He could have at least warned her that he told Dylan. Leaving their son to do his own dirty work.

"Shoot," she says again as she feels more tears fall down her cheeks.

Her phone says 4:09; they are still waiting for a couple groomsmen, so the photographers are running much later than schedule. At the moment, Leah doesn't think there is anything she can do. She turns away from the group to try to dry her tears and compose herself. She focuses on watching the photographer and putting Dylan out of her mind.

4:37pm Kristy

"ALRIGHT, GUYS." Kristy struggles to be heard over the din of the laughing and joking and ass slapping.

What is it with guys and ass slapping?

"Hey! Gentlemen? It's after four thirty. Let's do this quick and I'll release you to the bar!"

The groom and groomsmen had trickled in over the previous forty minutes. Slowly. Striding up the long driveway, many of them carrying their tux jackets instead of wearing them because it's already so hot. Excuses of traffic and wives and kids and at least two of them smell like Taco Bell. The blond one named Blake and the tall one — Kristy thinks his name is Ricky — are doing her job of scolding the others. Even the groom is getting a good-natured telling off.

"Stu! Get the fuck off the phone, bro!" Blake calls. The other groomsman has wandered back down the driveway, trying to find a quiet place to talk to his wife.

The boys are all here, but she still has not been able to get them started. Forget the fact that she intended to have finished these photos about ten minutes ago so she can move on to some family photos before the ceremony starts.

Chaos. Just like every other wedding.

Kristy just watches the boys for a few seconds, picking up on names and power dynamics. Ian is the loud one (and the bride's brother), and there's Ricky, Jason, Stuart and two more whose names she doesn't catch. Blake is the quiet one. The bride's other brother and blond like Lindsay. There's always at least one groomsman she can recruit to be on her side and relay instructions for her. She'll count on Blake to be that one if she needs it. A couple of the bridesmaids have come down to watch — their boyfriends or husbands evidently also being members of the wedding party — but having an audience does not help. Ian seems to know exactly where they stand and plays it up for their benefit. At least Marta is getting good shots. She can quietly and stealthily get candid pictures through this mess.

Once she is sure they have all said their hellos, Kristy picks out Ryan. He's enjoying his wedding, and doesn't seem to be anxious, which makes her job a little easier. She puts one hand on his arm to get his attention and flashes her most charming smile.

"Ryan? You ready? Can you come over here, please?"

She poses him against a backdrop of the house, and takes a step back.

The afternoon light is peeking over the top of the house at just the perfect angle. If she positions Ryan right … here, the whitewash texture of the building adds interest to the background, the backlight shines perfectly and the bougainvillea creeping up the wall frames the subject. Perfect.

She takes a couple simple groom-only shots to test the light and then Kristy calls to the others.

"Boys! C'mere and fill in around Ryan!"

Seven tipsy twenty-something men stumble in her direction. Again with the ass slapping. They certainly can not pose themselves, so Kristy takes a minute to change places, direct chins and hands. Make Ian take off his sunglasses.

Every weekend is the exact same story with a different cast.

Every group of groomsmen she photographs is a variation on this theme. If she were an anthropologist, or somehow disconnected it could be fascinating. The ritual? The roles? The way personalities can change simply because it is a wedding day?

But as it is, the whole situation annoys her. They are adults. She should not have to tell at least one person every single weekend to spit out his gum. Does he think she can't see him through her camera?

Kristy steps back to confer with Marta. They will not get another chance at this ever, so they need to make sure it was right. Nothing weird in the background? Does the group look balanced? Is the light hitting them from a flattering angle?

Ian makes some joke that she doesn't hear. Ryan calls to his dad to bring him another beer. Only Blake stands quietly, waiting for Kristy.

Blake is her favorite.

"Ok, guys, ready? You look great! You feel pretty? I'm just going to take a bunch of photos so keep smiling 'til I tell you to stop. Only look at my camera. I don't care who is behind me. Ready? Look at me!"

Kristy leans forward slightly so the camera is lower and the guys' proportions would be correct in the image. As she does, she hears Ian crack another joke.

"Yeah, look at her jugs! Right below the camera, ha ha! An old photographer's trick."

Kristy's heart thumps.

She hears nothing else. She has no idea if anyone laughs at the 'joke.'

What just happened?

There is a beat of silence before she responds, trying to sound light-hearted but still not removing her face from behind the camera.

"Yeah, well, if that makes you smile at the camera."

Kristy barely hears a small smattering of laughter around her as she finishes up a couple more shots. She stands up straight. She feels like all eyes are on her, staring at her chest. She tugs at the neck of her dress, worried that it is too low. She had deliberately added a layer of a tank top underneath her dress to make the neckline higher, but obviously that doesn't matter to this pig.

"Ok, um." She's flustered and can't remember what she needs to do next. "Marta? Do you have the shot list?"

Marta hurries forward, folded paper in hand. "You ok?" she whispers as they bent their heads together over the list.

"I guess. What an ass. But, really?"

"I know, I'm sorry."

Kristy takes a deep breath to reorient herself. Ok, shots with each individual groomsman now. She can do this. She flashes her charming smile again and steps forward to direct the drunks.

4:49pm Amber

THAT IDIOT IS JUST STANDING THERE on the lawn checking his phone. As soon as it is clear the photographer no longer needs him, Amber walks over to Ian and punches him in the arm.

"Hey!" he says, actually taking his sunglasses off to look at her.

"What is wrong with you? You can't just say that to people!"

"What's wrong with you? Why'd you punch me?"

"You can't talk to the photographer like that."

"Like what?"

"Oh for christsake. Do you have any idea what I'm talking about? How can you not remember?"

"Remember what? You're acting crazy."

"Ian. You told everyone here to look at the photographer's 'jugs.'"

"I did not."

"You absolutely did. Ask anyone. I cannot believe you."

"Why?" He grins. "You jealous?"

Amber rolls her eyes. Again, last night's mistake comes back to haunt her. "No, I'm not jealous. I'm appalled. You shouldn't say that to anyone. Let alone a stranger. A stranger who is currently working for your sister."

"Relax. I'm sure she thought it was funny. It's not a big deal."

"It is a big deal, you idiot. Do you know it is actually in her contract that she can leave if she is harassed by guests? And then Ryan and Lindsay are screwed. You may have just totally fucked up everything."

Ian stares at her, either unbelieving that she is telling the truth or unbelieving that she is making such a big deal. With Ian it could be either.

"And then you would owe them the few thousand dollars they spent on photography," Amber continues.

He puts his hands up in surrender. "Ok, ok. I get it. I was bad." He grins.

"Ugh. You are hopeless."

"No, really. I'll take care of it. But I've been meaning to talk to you, too." Amber dreads whatever is coming next. "So …. Last night?"

"Thank you for the ride last night. And that is all."

"Do you need a ride home tonight?"

"No. Go apologize to the photographer."

"Hey, hey." He tries to take her hand. "Don't change the subject. You look hot in that dress, by the way."

"Ian. Just … stop. Last night was a mistake. Do not talk to me about it again. And go apologize."

Amber walks away. He calls after her but she ignores him. He is not her responsibility. It is not her turn to babysit him. Let Blake or Ryan handle it. She knows from experience, Ian is exactly the kind of guy that will disregard anything any female tries to tell him. Trying to help him learn how to drive had been a joke.

Once more she reminds herself how stupid the previous night had been. *You're a fool, Amber*, she tells herself.

4:52pm Ian

IAN WATCHES AMBER WALK AWAY. Overreacting. Typical. She has always been overdramatic.

There's no way she's right, he thinks. *The photographer chick can't just leave. Even if I did say something.*

A few feet away, she photographs Ryan by himself, contorting her body at weird angles. As Ian watches, she straightens up and pulls on the neckline of her dress. She glances at him and blushes. He grins; he loves having that effect on girls.

Amber can't possibly be right. He wonders if the photographer is single. She probably would welcome an excuse to take a break and talk to him, right?

But then there's also Amber. If he gives her the attention she wants, he can hook up again with her tonight. But on the other hand there is also one other single bridesmaid who he has barely spoken to and who knows who else will show up as a guest. God, too many choices.

Ian grins. He needs to focus his energy. Nothing will happen if he tries to go after all of them.

He watches the photographer for a little while longer. She is conferring with the other one. They seem to be just waiting. Maybe now is a good time to go talk to her.

Before he can make up his mind to go do it, Ian spots Amber on the other side of the crowd talking to Blake. They are both looking at him.

Ian is a little irritated at the bridesmaid dresses. Lindsay should have told him. The whole thing doesn't match his groomsmen fantasy expectation at all. Far too sombre and too much fabric. Maybe that's what Amber's problem is — she hates her dress.

Ian decides to ignore whatever Blake and Amber are saying about him. He looks around quickly. No else notices him and no one seems to be telling him to do anything, so he makes another trip to the bar before they do.

5:09pm Sophie

"SOPH, read me the address again, please."

"18453 Pendleton Lane." Sophie tries to look at all the houses on either side of the street, but her mom drives too fast. They are all so big and fancy. They must be big enough for, like, three or four families to live in. The driveways are big enough for, maybe, ten cars, probably. She doesn't think she has ever been in a neighborhood like this before. She wonders if they have pools or if the kids that live in these houses have TVs in their bedrooms. There would be plenty of room for a dog if she lived in a house like this.

"Did you remember to grab my phone charger again, Soph?"

Sophie feels her eyes get wide. "Um, no Mom. Sorry."

Her mom sighs loudly. "Damn it, Sophie." Great-grandpa looks at her, startled. "Alright. Fine. Maybe Ryan will have one I can borrow real quick."

Sophie keeps quiet while her mom peers at each address on the right side of the street.

"Here it is," she says triumphantly, pulling into the driveway.

The long gravel driveway makes a funny crunching sound under the car tires. Sophie tries to peer out the window to see what it looks like.

"Ok, I'm going to drop you two off so you don't have to walk so far and then go park the car."

"Thanks, Mom."

"Yes, thank you, Karen, dear."

"Of course," she pats Great-grandpa's hand. "Sophie, it's already after five so be sure you tell Ryan and Lindsay you're sorry you're late. Tell them there was traffic. There's always traffic."

Most of her family is standing in front of the house. Some are having their photos taken. Some are just standing around and talking, drink in hand. Sophie can only remember the names of about half of the people she can see. She wishes her mom were with her, but the car is already about to pull onto the street. Sophie takes her great-grandfather's hand and walks with him slowly over to where most of the crowd stands. She feels shy and scared all of a sudden. Why hadn't she thought to ask about pictures? Does she have to do anything special? Is everyone going to be staring at her?

A lady dressed all in black and holding a big camera came up to her. "Hi, I'm Marta. Are you Sophie?"

Sophie nods.

"Well, Sophie, I really like your dress. Is this your grandpa?"

"Great-grandfather," he says, shaking her hand. "Marshall Page."

"Really? Wow. Nice to meet you. It's so great you're here. We should be ready for you for photos any second. Sophie, I'm going to let Kristy who is the other photographer know you're here ok? Mr. Page, can I get you a chair or water or something?"

Sophie doesn't hear the rest of the conversation. She wanders a few steps away, watching a bunch of boys hanging around her mom's cousin Ryan. They are all dressed alike, except there is one wearing sunglasses.

She clasps her hands together, ducking her head slightly to try to stay small and invisible. Those boys look like they're having fun and she wants to hear what they are doing.

"Ian. Dude, hey." Sophie watches the tallest boy walk over to the one wearing sunglasses and hit him gently in the arm. "You got the stuff? For the car?"

"Huh?"

They're both whispering, but not very quietly. Sophie can still hear all of it. They keep looking at Ryan, though. Probably to make sure he can't hear anything.

"The pens. The balloons. Did you get the stuff?"

"Oh. Shit. … No."

"Come on, Ian. I asked you to do one thing!"

"I know. And I went there. I just … I dunno. Got distracted?"

"You got distracted? At a party supply store."

"Oh, is that what they sold?" The grin under his sunglasses widens. "'Cause I just left with this girl's number."

"You are unbelievable," the tall boy says, shaking his head. "This is your sister's wedding. Do you care about other people at all?"

"C'mon. It's not that big of a deal."

"Oh, really? Ok. Well you tell your sister that her only wedding is not that big a deal."

"Fuck, I'm sorry, okay?" Ian says as the other one walks away.

"Sophie?"

She starts — did someone hear that boy say the f-word? The lady named Marta stands behind her, leaning down a bit to be on Sophie's eye level.

"You ready? Come over here, please. We're going to take a couple photos of you by yourself and then some in a group, ok?"

Sophie follows, nervous and excited. The crowd has changed since she started watching Ryan and his friends. But she still doesn't see her mom.

5:29pm Marshall

MARSHALL IS grateful for the ride, but even more grateful to be out of the car. He has never approved of the way his grand-daughter speaks around her child. He stands in the grass, waiting to be needed.

The bride is already hidden away. Guests are arriving, but the schedule seems to be running late. That must be the wedding coordinator hovering behind the photographer, ready to snag the groom as soon as possible.

Marshall has just taken a couple quick photos with Ryan. One of the photographers has asked him to return to this spot after the ceremony for more family photos. Marshall tries to pay attention and follow directions, but the laughing and joking of his grandsons distracts him. They smell like beer and ignore him.

But, the photographer has been so sweet to him. She has gone to find him a chair so he won't have to stand in the sun too long. Marshall hates to be treated like a fragile old person, but sometimes it's necessary that he give in. He has already been up for so long and had many hours to go.

A teenage boy dressed in black carries a chair toward him.

"Are you the grandfather?"

Marshall shrugs. "Do you see any other old farts?"

The boy smiles, politely. Marshall isn't making much of a joke. "Where would you like to sit, sir? On the grass under the tree? Out there in the sun where you can watch what they're doing?"

Marshall shrugs again. It doesn't really matter.

"What about right here? By the path. You're still in the shade, but everyone will be able to see you. My name is Dylan, so when you all are done here just have someone come find me and I'll take the chair. I'll be in the back working with the caterer."

"Thank you, Dylan. That's very kind. You and the photographer have both been so thoughtful already."

"Really?" Dylan looks surprised. "Isn't this your family?"

"Oh, yes. But they all have their own lives now. They have other things to worry about, I'm sure. My granddaughter who brought me hasn't even acknowledged me since she parked the car."

Dylan forehead wrinkles down toward his eyes. "Really?"

"Yes. But don't worry about me, son." Marshall pats Dylan's hand that rests on the back of the chair. "I'm used to being alone. After my parents, and then my wife died I've had more and more time to get used to it."

"Your parents? How long has that been?"

"Oh, a while." Marshall pauses, remembering. "Yes, quite awhile. And my wife eleven years ago this summer. But, in my experience your parents and your spouse are the only people in the world who love you whole-heartedly and unreservedly. Your siblings, maybe. I suppose. Your kids, maybe. When they think of it. But your parents brought you into this life and want you to be happy."

Dylan listens quietly.

"Of course, there are exceptions," Marshall says, watching his granddaughter Karen flirt with one of the groomsmen in sunglasses. He shakes himself out of his reverie. "I'm sorry, son. I'm just jabbering away. It isn't often that someone actually stops to talk to me. Forgive me. I know you must have work to do."

"Thank you, sir. It was really nice to meet you."

"My name is Marshall Page. It was nice to meet you too."

"Seriously, though. Do you need anything else before I go, Mr. Page? Water? Burrito? Beer?"

Marshall laughs a little. It feels like a muscle that hadn't been used in years. "No, thank you. I'll find you when I'm done with the chair."

"Ok. See ya."

The boy walks away, back to the house where he no doubt has plenty more to do to prepare for the wedding. Many more important things than standing around talking to an old man. Just before he reaches the house, Marshall sees Dylan makes a sharp turn and walk toward where the bartender is setting up instead. The two boys turn toward Marshall; he sees Dylan pointing at him; the bartender nods and starts walking toward him, bottle of water in hand.

What a thoughtful young man, Marshall thinks. His mother must be so proud of him.

5:43pm Leah

LEAH WATCHES HER TALL, lanky son cross the lawn with his giant strides. Dylan stops by the bar instead of coming straight to Leah like she had asked. She frowns. Oh, but … From the way he points it looks like he is asking for something for a guest. That is okay then. As long as that was all.

"Hey, Mom. What else do you need?"

Leah tries not to show that she is surprised. He is still sullen, and he might not realize it but a lot of the anger has gone out of his tone. She blinks a couple times. "Um. Oh, nothing, dear. Thank you. The ceremony is about to start."

He just nods and keeps walking, back to where the rest of the waiters keep out of sight until dinner.

Leah watches him, unable to help thinking about how much he looks like his father. She has always loved that fact before, but today it just seems unnecessarily cruel. Taunting her, almost.

DJ Dick Hannigan approaches her, hand out-stretched to shake hers. "Mrs. Holder? Are we close? Looks like the last of the guests are making their way to their seats."

Mrs. Holder. How much longer will people call her that?

She checks the time on her phone: 5:43pm. How is it

possible they are almost on time after the photography ran so late? Kristy must be really good. Leah turns back to Dick. "Yes. Just a couple minutes. I'll check that everyone is in place."

She finds the groomsmen first. It's not difficult, since they are all within about ten feet of the bar.

"It's time, gentleman. Can I get you to go around to the front of the house? It's time. Are you ready? Follow Blake around to the front." She moves swiftly between the men, whispering, gesturing, calmly directing them to where she needs them to be.

The younger one in the sunglasses is the only hold-out.

"Hi! Ian, right?" she says. "Ready? It's time to start. I need you to follow the others, please."

"Yeah, ok," he says, turning away from her. He turns his back completely to Leah, stays right where he was and continues to drink his beer.

"Um, I'm sorry." She walks around to be standing in front of him again. "You can take that with you, but I need you to go to the front of the house, please."

She puts her hand on his arm not holding the beer and he finally looks at her. Surprised, almost, to see her standing there. "Alright, alright."

He swallows the last of his beer in one long gulp, tosses the bottle in the trash on top of several others, and slowly begins his way over to where he is supposed to be.

"And take off your sunglasses before it starts, please," she calls after him. He gives no indication that he heard.

Leah sighs. At least the bridesmaids would be easier; they should all be inside still.

Leah cuts across the tiled patio, weaving in between the last trickle of guests, and slips into the kitchen via the side door. The room is mostly dark, just one overhead light on above the sink. No one has really been in this part of the house for hours. All the lights are off. As Leah cuts the corner through the living room, she comes across a little eight-year-old sitting alone on the couch.

"Oh! Goodness, you scared me! Sophie? Sweetheart? Where's your mom? Why are you in here all alone?"

The little girl shrugs.

"Oh. Well. Ok. It's almost time to walk down the aisle. Are you ready? You're a big girl. I think you can handle it, right? Do you know what you are supposed to do right now?" Where is this child's mother? Leah was not hired to be a babysitter, even if Sophie seems used to taking care of herself.

"Yes, ma'am."

"Great. That is wonderful, sweetheart. You have your basket, right? Can you just go out front where the groomsmen are? We'll walk from there."

She shrugs again, but slides down off the couch and starts toward the front door without a word.

One last excursion upstairs to the master bedroom. Lindsay and all her girls should be up there. They had better all be up there. Leah reaches the door and raps quickly. "Girls! It's time!"

The maid of honor opens the door. "Ready? Ok. We're coming. Lindsay!" she calls over her shoulder.

Leah steps out of the way as six lovely girls in black started filing out of the bedroom door, chattering to each other, laughing, checking that their hair is still in place.

"Amber, please be sure you remind Lindsay to give you her bouquet when she gets to the altar. And can you please just give her a once over? Make sure everything is tucked in that needs to be? Thank you so much."

She hurries back downstairs to direct the rest of the wedding party in the processional. Ryan, bless him, is already at the altar, so she only has to release the pairs to walk at reasonable intervals.

"Gum out. All of you. Here, give it to me." She moves from groomsman to groomsman, prompting them to show her their mouths are empty or spit it into her hand if not.

The DJ sees her in place around the corner of the house, and with a nod from Leah, plays the music.

It begins.

They all get off smoothly, albeit at different paces. *This is why we have a rehearsal, people*, she thinks. Then comes Lindsay, almost floating and gloriously beautiful. The ideal bride. Leah is as proud as if Lindsay had been her daughter.

Finally they are all down the aisle, in their places, and Leah can watch from the back of the crowd.

"Who gives this woman to be wed?"

She feels punched in the gut. Leah turns away, breathless and surprised at her reaction. She can't help it. She can't handle it. Her calm, stoic demeanor she has held the entire day cracks under the reality of the situation. She has been able to forget about her own problems in the rush of doing her job, but now that she has a moment to herself it comes rushing back.

The vows are coming. The eternal vows, promising to love each other for the rest of their lives. Love each other and not separate and not turn their children against the other.

Shoot.

Leah thinks she can slip away for just a minute. Pastor Roberts has the ceremony all under control for at least fifteen minutes. Without thinking, Leah slips her hand into her pocket and wraps her fingers around her cell phone. She's tired of pretending she doesn't care; she's going to try to call Joe.

To heck with her usual rules. If any situation deserves an exception, this is it. Leah hurries into the house; the dining room should be empty again as long as everyone is outside.

She immediately finds her favorites list and presses 'call,' holding the phone to her ear as she walks. Nothing.

She hangs up before Joe's outgoing message finishes.

Maybe a text? "Do you have a minute to talk?" Send.

Nothing.

Leah takes a breath and tries calling again.

"Hi, um. It's, uh ... It's me," she stammers into the voicemail. "I just had a really quick minute to call and see ... uh. I guess, how your day is going? Or, um. If you maybe had thought about, uh... If you had, had thought any more about what you decided. And, um, maybe wondering if you had changed your mind? I'm sorry. I'm rambling. I just ... I just wanted to talk if you had a minute. I, uh ... I have go back to work. Ok, bye."

She hangs up frantically, as if the sooner she presses end the better her message would sound.

But she doesn't have time for any more indulgences. She is supposed to be working. The ceremony is still going on and there is a chance she will be needed.

Leah wipes the tears from her face, returns her still silent phone to her pocket and leaves the house.

5:50pm Dylan

DYLAN STANDS in the very back, behind the last row of chairs, deep in the shade on the side of the house, hidden between tall shrubbery. He watches his mom duck into the house, phone to her ear. He has never seen her make a personal call or text while working — she has always been very firm on that point. There's probably some wedding disaster that she needs to fix.

Dylan wonders what she had done that morning when his dad told her he was moving out. It must have killed her to have someone make a decision she had not been part of. Dylan always thinks 'controlling' isn't a strong enough word to describe his mom.

He tries to picture his parents' wedding and can't. He just keeps getting an image of his mom doing her coordinating job, but in a wedding dress, with some other faceless bride by his dad's side having all the fun. If there is one thing he has learned from the few weddings he worked, it's that the brides who let go of control and making everything perfect always have the most fun (a lesson he immediately carried over to his skateboarding, even after he broke his collarbone).

He can not imagine his mother ever letting go of control. She must have hated her wedding day.

Dylan's mom has not yet emerged from the house. It occurs to him that maybe she's actually breaking her own rule. Maybe she's trying to call Joe, and he wonders if his dad has picked up the phone. He doubts it. He could have told his mom not to bother. Dad is totally set on this. His stuff was mostly packed by ten that morning, for god's sake.

The pastor continues talking. Preaching, Dylan supposes. About love and marriage and what it all means. They haven't gotten to the rings or anything yet. Dylan watches the one groomsman who had left his sunglasses on mouth something to someone in the audience. What a tool. What is that guy even doing in this wedding party? He doesn't seem like he belongs at all. He must be related somehow. A duty groomsman.

Dylan doesn't have any siblings. He wonders abstractedly who he might have in his own wedding one day. He wonders if his parents would remain civil after they separate, if they would both be pleasant at his graduation next year, or his wedding sometime later in the future.

Dylan doesn't really want to have to choose between them. Especially because if he has the option he will totally choose his dad. But Dylan isn't sure he will be given the option and, if he does choose his dad, it will probably crush his mother. It would totally go against how she sees herself, as a mother and as a wedding coordinator. It's like she would not know who she is without those two things. If Dylan chooses his dad, she will lose half of her purpose in life. Her value. In her mind, at least.

He's angry with her, but he isn't sure he can do that to her.

Dylan's mind wanders back to what the old grandpa had said. About family. And about being alone. He hadn't seemed too keen on his own, but they don't seem to care about him much either.

Dylan rubs his temple and closes his eyes. The June heat

gives him a headache. Fighting with his mom doesn't help. But goddamn is she a pain sometimes.

She creeps out of the house at that moment, clearly guilty she had left the ceremony site and glances around side-eyed to see if anyone has noticed, anyone whose opinion she values. She never sees Dylan staring right at her.

5:53pm Ian

THIS IS THE WORST, Ian thinks. *Standing in the fucking sun while his sister babbles on? I am taking this jacket off at the earliest possible moment.* The wedding party and pastor are positioned just slightly higher than the guests on a small hill up against the fence, so Ian can see the whole crowd.

That Karen girl he had noticed earlier is watching Ian instead of the bride and groom. She catches his eye and gives him a half smile before tossing her hair back over her shoulder. He chuckles to himself, grinning back. He would talk to her as soon as this thing was over. He thinks she has a kid, but there is a ton of other family around and it's a fucking backyard wedding. The little girl will be fine on her own for a little while.

The main photographer crouches in the aisle, photographing the ceremony. Ian had not noticed her there; she must have been doing her job from the back or around the side. She glances up at him, but looks away without acknowledging.

Goddamn, this is the perfect angle to see down her dress, Ian thinks. *She's just asking for it.*

After another few moments, she gets up and walks back up the aisle ruining his view. Ian tries to look around covertly. What are the other guys doing? Everyone seems to be listening intently. Ian sighs and turns his attention back to his sister.

He doesn't have any idea what was happening in the ceremony. He vaguely remembers the coordinator lady saying that music would be playing when they walk back up the aisle, so Ian is kind of just waiting for that.

Now the other photographer is in the aisle, also crouched down and photographing the bride and groom. Ian wonders where the main girl went.

Oh well. This is almost done.

And then he has to take a few more photos.

Then open bar the rest of the night — the best reason to be here.

Sure, he loves Lindsay. And, yes, Ryan is an awesome brother-in-law. But this whole wedding thing? The fancy outfits and all the rules? Totally not his thing. Ian would not at all have been offended to not be invited.

But since he has been, he will absolutely take advantage of it. He has a strong suspicion he will be able to find that Karen girl near the bar as soon as the ceremony is over. Ian grins when he notices she is still looking at him.

5:55pm Amber

AMBER HOLDS the bride's bouquet. *No wonder the bride always hands it off*, she thinks. *This thing is heavy.* Must be almost two dozen dense, pink rosebuds, in addition to all the greenery and filler.

"For better or for worse. For rich or for poor."

Lindsay and Amber had had a long conversation about the wedding vows. Were those old traditional vows too staid? Too old fashioned? But, on the other hand, did Lindsay think she could write anything better?

Amber tries to stand up straighter and focus on what is being said. So she can gush appropriately later. Her best friend in the whole world vows to love this really great guy forever and ever. Amber knows she should be focused and attentive and maybe even cry because she is so happy for Lindsay. But she can't.

Mostly because she's so hot. The sun is still out in full force and somebody had miscalculated. All of the guests are in the shade of the house, but the altar and entire wedding party swelter in direct sun. Whose idea was these black bridesmaid dresses? Amber can feel the sweat rolling down her back. The dress will be sticking to her any second, and everyone will see her dark sweat spots as she walks back up the aisle.

If the minister doesn't hurry up Amber is sure she'll be dripping make-up onto the front of her black dress.

Amber tries to covertly blow her bangs up. Even her warm breath is a little bit cooler than her skin.

In those few seconds when she isn't distracted by the heat, Amber has to remember to avoid eye contact with Ian. They have always been friendly before last night, so it's a little weird for her to be avoiding him. It's easy, though, since he had smuggled his sunglasses up to the altar. And he is apparently talking to someone in the audience.

She should have eaten more. Lunch feels like so long ago. Amber bends her knees just a tiny bit — the coordinator had warned all the wedding party about locking their knees and fainting during the ceremony. The ceremony feels unnaturally long. They hadn't run through the whole thing at the rehearsal the previous night, so Amber isn't totally certain what to expect.

"Ryan, I am so thankful for every day you are in my life."

Amber has heard Lindsay's vows. She wrote at least a third of them. Ryan's vows are a surprise, though.

"Lindsay, for all the time I have known you, you have been nothing short of perfect."

Amber's throat tightens. Tears well up.

Why is Amber still alone? What's wrong with her?

She hears Pastor Roberts pronouncing them man and wife. She hears the cheers and applause as Ryan dips Lindsay for their kiss. She feels herself smiling manically as she senses herself being on display, cameras clicking from all directions.

6:11pm Kristy

AS THE BRIDE and groom walk back up the aisle, Kristy checks her phone — 6:11pm. Only eleven minutes off schedule. Not terrible. She hopes Leah can hold dinner for the little bit of time they need.

The guests pour into the aisle behind the wedding party, shuffling their way toward cocktails and appetizers. Marta makes her way around the edge of the crowd.

"Do you want me to shoot the cocktail hour photos?"

Kristy thinks about that for a moment. What it would mean. What it would leave for her to do. That had been the original plan, but ...

"Marta, what lens do you have on right now?"

"Um, 35?"

"Ok, perfect. I'd like you to handle the big group shots if you don't mind? I don't want to give that pig any other reason to look at me." She tugs at the neckline of her tank top.

"Oh my god, of course. I still cannot believe he said that. Of course, whatever you need."

"Thank you." Kristy smiles. She wants to cry. She tips her head back and waits a beat to get control of her tears.

"I'll go get started. Before that asshole has another beer." Marta pats her arm before walking toward the bar.

Kristy watches her wind her way through the crowd to try to corral the groomsmen. Thank god for Marta.

The more she thinks about it, the more Kristy marvels at the fact that she had been able to come up with a retort so quickly. She's tougher than she thought. Of all the weddings she has shot she has never, ever been made to feel like that. Like she is on display for some jerk's gaze instead of being hired for her skills. Like she is the butt of some disgusting joke.

She wants to call Nick right away and tell him … but she also doesn't want him to know. Ever. It's all so embarrassing. But he would want to know. She texts him. Just a quick note: 'Awful day. Groomsman made a comment about my boobs. I'll tell you about it when I get home.'

She stares at her phone, scrolling through Instagram for a full two or three minutes to distract herself while she wills him to respond.

Nothing.

The crowd has thinned and Leah's team is already taking down the rows of chairs where guests sat to watch the ceremony. Kristy sighs and makes her way around the edge of the patio where the guests are hugging and exclaiming over Lindsay and Ryan. They still have not made it through to where Marta has the rest of the wedding party waiting.

Kristy stops and puts a hand on Lindsay's arm, waiting to get her attention.

"Oh! Yes! Here I come. I'm so sorry!" Lindsay smiles at Kristy, says good-bye, again, to the older couple she had been talking to, grabs Ryan's hand and follows behind the photographer to the front yard where the large group photos will be taken.

It takes a few minutes to get everyone organized. Ryan has a huge family; probably a third of the guests are related to him. Kristy works on directing and posing, and leaves the actual photography to Marta. Once that side of the family is done, and they move on to Lindsay's family, Kristy is more hesitant. She deliberately avoids eye contact with Ian and instead directs everyone around him.

While Marta photographs the grandparents, Kristy hangs back in the shade of the front of the house. The low hedge around the front stoop obscures her just enough to let her be forgotten.

But Blake must have been looking for her specifically. As soon as he spots her, he comes to meet her. His slow steps belie his single-minded intention. He stands on the lawn and talks to her over the hedge. "I, uh… I apologize for my brother Ian. He's had a lot to drink. I'm sure he doesn't realize how rude he is being."

"Thank you."

It takes some effort, but she manages to not roll her eyes. She won't let herself smile or do any of those little expressions to downplay and assure the other person it is okay. It's not okay. It's undoubtedly awkward for Blake, but, really, making excuses for such behavior is almost as insulting. She wants everyone to forget about it, even though she never will.

Blake smiles sheepishly and backs away a couple steps.

Kristy needs this day to be over. It had started with nerves and being disappointed she couldn't stay home with Nick, but it has only gotten worse. There is only have about three and a half hours left. But who's counting?

As Marta finishes up with all the large family photos, Kristy notices Ian trying to catch her eye. She steadfastly refuses to acknowledge his existence. She will have to remind Marta to make sure Ian is in some of her shots, because Kristy will not be pointing her camera in his direction.

Her phone buzzes. A response from Nick: 'What???! Want me to come down there? I'm sorry, babe. Can't wait to see you.'

Kristy smiles. Only three hours left if you don't count her break for dinner.

6:28pm Ian

IAN STANDS for a moment to the side of the bar, Coke in hand. No beer for now. If Amber was right, he's got to get a bit under control. He scans the patio and the rest of the backyard, looking for a woman dressed all in black. Unfortunately there are several — all of the bridesmaids, two photographers and at least three waitresses. But, there she is. The hot one wearing the dress with the low neckline. Standing at a cocktail table not far away looking at the back of her camera. Her back is to him, so she will not see him coming. Ian rolls his shoulders, and stretches his neck. Relax, he thinks as he tries to walk over to her as casually as possible.

"Hey."

She looks up. A flash of ... something, crosses her face before she gives him a half smile. "Hello."

She returns her attention to her camera. Goddamnit, she's not going to make this easy for him is she? He stares into his cup.

"Great wedding, right?"

"Sure."

"How late will you be here?"

She looks at him, narrowing her eyes. "Ten."

"Cool."

Silence. *Fuck.*

"You, uh … You should have a drink. You and the other girl have been working really hard."

She narrows her eyes at him, waiting a second before responding. "I am not going to drink while I'm working. Which reminds me…" She offers him a tight, cold, not-quite-a-smile, holds up her camera so he can see she's working, and walks away.

No good-bye. No apologetic smile. No nice to meet you. She just walks away from him.

Well fuck her then, he thinks. *I come over here and try to be a nice guy and smooth things over and she just walks away?*

Ian finishes the rest of his Coke in one big gulp and walks back to the bar for the real drink he deserves.

7:00pm Amber

THE LINE at the bar is still at least a dozen people deep. Amber sits at the head table alone, watching the guests, watching the coordinator and the DJ chatting. They're both looking around, gesturing. Discussing something specific, it looks like. Leah points at Amber, and the DJ nods.

Here it comes, she thinks.

Only about a third of the chairs around the tables are filled when the DJ goes into action. He's tall and middle-aged, still-dark hair that probably had some help. She watches as he goes out of his way to talk to every single person standing on the dance floor, interrupting their conversation and handing them his card, during cocktail hour.

Great choice for a wedding DJ.

"Alright everyone," he announces from the middle of the dance floor. "Let's all find our seats. Get our drinks. The party is about to begin!"

Amber rolls her eyes, although she supposes it's his job. He seems to be having fun, and she knows Ryan and Lindsay love his cheesiness, so at least there's that.

"Ladies and gentleman, please put your hands together for the happy couple: Mr. and Mrs. Ryan and Lindsay Rowe!"

They appear from around the side of the house. Not a particularly grand entrance, but options are limited in a back-yard. The awkward DJ continues to chatter — how lovely she looks, how lucky they are — but Amber has tuned him out. She watches her best friend be led to the middle of the dance floor by her new husband as Etta James starts crooning through the speakers.

The DJ catches her eye and begins moving toward her through the crowd. *Oh, god,* she thinks. *I guess that's me.*

"You're the maid of honor?"

"Yes." She tries to smile welcomingly. She really is trying.

"You ready for your toast when they're done dancing?"

"I guess."

"Ok, great. We're doing this first dance and then straight into toasting. You go first, then hand it off to the best man."

"Ok." Amber looks around. Where is Ricky? He had better not leave her standing here with a mic.

As the dance progresses, more and more guests find their seats, carefully squeezing between other tables where guests have pulled their chairs out into the aisle. She spots Ricky, waving a bit to catch his eye and gesture him over. He kisses his wife and helps her into her chair at a nearby table, then joins Amber and the rest of the wedding party.

As soon as he sits, she leans over to whisper, "Are you ready for your toast?"

"Sure. No problem."

She can't ask him any more because the song is ending, people are clapping, the DJ is talking.

Amber hears her name. This is it.

She stands up and clears her throat, holding the mic awkwardly. It is heavy and enormous in her hand. She feels every eye on her and is suddenly very aware that she is about to give a toast without having a drink in her hand.

"Shit," she whispers. But not quietly enough that it is not picked up by the microphone. Amber hears a small ripple of laughter around the tables as she looks for her glass. There are so many at this table; which is hers? She must look completely lost because Ricky reaches over to select the glass of champagne sitting between them and hands it to her.

Amber tries to communicate every ounce of gratitude in her body in just the look she gives him as she took her glass.

Ok, here we go.

"Um, hi," she says into the mic. The DJ adjusts the volume. "I'm Amber. I'm the maid of honor. I just wanted to thank everyone for coming tonight. I know Ryan and Lindsay feel very grateful that you all could make it."

And then she realizes that her speech is folded up and tucked in the ribbon wrapped around her bouquet.

Which is at that moment decorating the cake table all the way on the other side of the yard.

Her heart thumps, her face flushes, and for a second she stops breathing.

What did I write in that toast?

Every eye is on her, and she can already hear whispered conversations beginning at some of the farther away tables. She has lost them.

"I, uh … I've known Lindsay for about, um. Fifteen years? Almost? And I have never seen her as happy with any of her past boyfriends as she has been these last two years with Ryan."

She catches the eye of Ryan's grandfather sitting at the closest table with the more of his family. The old man smiles as if whatever she is saying is the best thing he has heard all day.

"He is kind and generous and … They are both very lucky to have each other."

She looks at Lindsay, who is beaming at her, leaning snuggled against Ryan.

"I suppose this is where I tell Ryan if he hurts her I'll kill him." A light laughter murmurs through the crowd. "But I'm not worried about that. These two have what it takes to …" Her voice catches. She can't cry. Not now. "They have what it takes for the long run. I know they will compromise and take care of each other and just… Just be there for whatever the other one needs. Their marriage will be something we should all look to and hope to have for ourselves. If we can be so lucky."

She has got to wrap it up. The tears are spilling over.

"So, let's all raise our glass," she can barely get the words out. She clears her throat. "To Ryan and Lindsay. Congratulations, you guys." Amber turns to her best friend as she gestures with her glass of champagne. She hears clinking and shouts of 'congratulations' all around her, but she only has eyes for Lindsay. Her best friend who is going to be so deservedly happy, while Amber still wanders in the wilderness, single and sad.

"Love you," Lindsay whispers as she hugs Amber fiercely. "Thank you."

"Love you," Amber whispers back. She is completely unable to hide or stop the tears now. "I'm really so very happy for you."

7:22pm Leah

THE TOASTS FINISH UP, and they are only running a little late now. But Leah knows they can pick up some extra minutes during dinner. Ryan and Lindsay will be finished eating first and lead the way. Everything will be fine and she is in the home stretch.

Leah checks the time — 7:22pm and still no contact from Joe. She has guessed as much and is starting to feel insulted by his obvious avoidance of her. Even though she is at work all day, he could at least say something. Anything. It's rude to not even respond after she had called and texted. 'All packed up and ready to leave,' 'Got to my sister's, I'll call you tomorrow.' Anything.

Leah wonders if Dylan has heard from his father. Probably. They have always been a lot closer than she and Dylan. Or sometimes even closer than she and Joe.

They constantly make plans without her — "Sorry, hon'. We assumed you would be working." Dylan would only call for his mom if he needs something like a ride or to tell them he'd be late. They have inside jokes without her. They somehow both went to see the latest Coen brothers movie and she still doesn't know where she was when that happened.

For a long time now, Leah has been feeling like an outsider in her own family.

Leah bristles. She doesn't have time for this. She has to get nearly one-hundred people served dinner within, ideally, the next ten to fifteen minutes. It's possible, but it requires focus. No more wondering what her husband is doing or thinking. She needs to make her clients the priority.

Which means taking care of the vendors, too. She needs help. A waiter.

"Dylan!" She catches his arm as he walks by. "Can you make sure the DJ, the two photographers, the make-up artist and ... I think that's it. Can you make sure they all get dinner? Please? I believe the vendor meals are stacked in the back for them."

"Ok."

"And tell them they can eat in the dining room inside. Plenty of room and no one will bother them. Do you need me to show you where it is?"

"I can probably figure it out, right?" His tone makes it clear he is a bit insulted that she thinks he needs help finding a dining room.

"Oh, yes. You're right. I'm sure you can." Leah backs off. She needs to remind herself to start giving him his space. Especially if he decides he wants that space to be at Joe's new home.

As soon as he has gone again, Leah mentally ticks off the final tasks she has to worry about throughout the rest of the evening. More dancing, cake, bouquet, garter, money dance if there is time. Quick mental calculations: If we can get everyone done by dinner by 8, 8:15 at the latest that should be perfect. All of the vendors will leave at ten, so they would have about two hours to accomplish it all. No problem. This wedding is running smoothly.

Dylan is suddenly at her elbow, hands full of styrofoam

containers. "Mom, there was one more vendor meal back there. Do you know whose it is?"

She stares at him. She stares past him, really, searching her brain for who she is neglecting.

"Is it yours, maybe?" he asks, after a few moments.

"Oh!" She laughs. "Yes, I suppose it is. Thank you, dear."

He gives her a confused look, hands her the dinner she had forgotten and leaves to go distribute the food.

As she watches him, she thinks how funny it is that Dylan is so similar to her in some respects but fights it tooth and nail. There's a reason she has found him a job with a caterer. He's a fantastic organizer and leader, adopting all of her best traits, but with a tender heart that he keeps hidden. She can imagine him a big important CEO one day, smart and capable and beloved by his employees, secretly paying off their mortgages or giving away vacations.

Of course, he would never admit he is so similar to his mother. That's not cool.

He'll handle this just fine, Leah thinks as she opens her dinner to eat a few quick bites.

7:30pm Kristy

ONCE THE TOASTS are over and the dinner is served, Kristy plucks at Marta's sleeve. "Let's go find dinner."

No one ever remembers to take care of the photographer, Kristy thinks. Where's Leah?

They have to weave their way through a few waiters, around some tables full of guests and then across the patio. As they approach the door into the kitchen, they almost run smack into a sixteen-year-old boy dressed in all black, with two takeout containers in his hands.

"Whoa! Sorry! I, uh. I think I'm supposed to look for you?" He eyes their attire, big camera bags still slung over their shoulders. "The photographers?"

"Yes, thank you." Kristy smiles.

"There's silverware in there, and I'm supposed to show you where the dining room is."

"Fantastic," Marta says from behind her.

As the boy leads them through the house, Marta says, "Once I shot a wedding at a church, and they stuck us in the nursery for dinner. We had to eat on the floor surrounded by cribs and teething rings."

"Ugh. That sounds awful." Marta is being chatty, but Kristy appreciates it. The other girl is clearly trying to take Kristy's mind off of the events of that afternoon.

They sit across from each other. The dining room is lit only by a brass chandelier with weak bulbs. There is a dark wood chair rail around the edge of the room with yellow, flowered wallpaper on the wall above. The whole room feels dark and yellow. Not exactly the most appetizing place to eat — no wonder it seems virtually unused since the house had been built.

Kristy opens her styrofoam box: roasted carrots, mashed potatoes and a small chicken breast in a cream sauce. Not pretty but not terrible. It could have been worse.

"This smells delicious," Marta says from behind her styrofoam lid.

"You think?" Kristy kind of loves how positive Marta is all the time. It's growing on her.

"Oh, yeah! Once I shot a wedding where we got sad sandwiches on Wonder Bread and those super syrupy fruit cups they give four year olds."

Kristy laughs. "Yeah, this is better."

They eat in silence for a minute or two. In spite of all the waiting around, neither of them has eaten anything for almost eight hours. Only two hours left after dinner, Kristy thinks. Only two hours left to stay out of Ian's presence.

"So, that pig Ian tried to talk to me."

"He did not! What did he say?"

"I'm not sure …. He either tried to hit on me or tried to apologize. It's not totally clear." She tries make light of it. Maybe it's funny from someone else's point of view. Maybe.

"I still can't believe he said that."

"I know. His brother apologized for him, but still."

"I think you handled it so well. I just froze up."

"Oh, thanks. My uncles are all joking and sarcastic, so I'm used to being quick with the comebacks." Her uncles would have kicked that guy's ass. She almost wishes her Uncle Ted were there to stand up for her.

Kristy starts crying. She should not feel so helpless. This fucking job.

"Oh my god, I'm so sorry. We can change the subject." Marta reaches out and takes her hand.

"It's okay. It's not your fault. It's just so … I'm so embarrassed. And so angry. I have never been treated like that while working a wedding. Ever. It's ruined everything."

Marta squeezes her hand without saying anything.

The flower girl sticks her head in the room. She could not be more than eight or nine years old — what is she doing wandering around by herself? Especially since there are so many of her relatives around to look out for her?

"Hi, hon'," Marta says, standing up. "Can I help you?"

"No, sorry," she mutters, chewing on a fingernail. Sophie, maybe? "Just lookin' for my mom." With that she's gone again.

"I don't know why I'm telling you this. I'm sorry."

"No no no! Of course, whatever you need. Who else are you going to talk to? It's not like your husband shoots weddings, right?"

"Yeah, I guess. It's just … it started out as a little thing. I hate having to work on a weekend when my husband is home. But then another little thing and another, and then it gets harder and harder to charge what makes it worth it to me. And then this today. I'm just so tired of it all."

Marta nods, and tries to look like she understands. Kristy knows it's pointless — there isn't anyone else she knows who would understand. Every wedding photographer she knows loves their job and everyone else in her life can not really understand the demands of the job.

She puts a big piece of carrot in her mouth and takes her time chewing. What if she does quit? What could she do instead?

Kristy's phone shakes the whole table as it vibrates with a

new text. It's from Nick: 'You okay? Want me to turn on the hot tub bubbles for when you get home?'

'Yes please'

He really is the best, Kristy thinks. *I just have to make it through two more hours of work.*

"Hey, Marta, quick question. When you shoot weddings, do you check the time a lot?"

"You mean, to, like, make sure you're on schedule?"

"More like how soon can I go home?"

Marta looks confused. "No, not really. At least a third of the time I end up staying an extra half an hour because I'm having fun."

"Really?" Kristy has never once stayed at a wedding longer than she was contracted to do. And she certainly is not going to start tonight.

"Sure. I mean, they're only going to have one wedding, right?"

"I guess."

They sit in silence, each eating quickly since they have to begin working again soon.

7:32pm Marshall

ONE OF THE waitresses had to help Marshall find his seat. There are place cards everywhere, but he had no idea where to start. He must have looked lost, so she offered her arm and led him straight to his prime spot at a family table closest to the bride and groom. One of the privileges of being old, he supposes. That and the fact that he isn't expected to dance. Once the ceremony had finished, and the other guests milled about while the chairs were moved to around the tables, Marshall had simply found his spot and rooted himself there, alone.

He doesn't expect Karen to stick by him the whole night, but since she is his ride home it would be nice if he at least knew where she is. He hasn't seen her since … since the ceremony when that obnoxious boy had attempted to flirt with her from the altar.

Marshall shakes his head. That boy is obviously trouble. And Karen doesn't seem to be able to tell the difference.

He had seated himself on the opposite side of the table from the dance floor, and has to crane his neck a bit to see over the centerpiece. Through the flower stems he scans the backyard.

He doesn't see Sophie anywhere either. Well, maybe she is with her mother, in which case he won't worry.

After all, no one seems to be worried about him. Two of his kids, plus their spouses, plus all their children and more, and not one of his relations is even sitting with him pretending to make conversation.

Marshall picks up his place card and rubs his thumb over the embossed name. He misses Carol so much.

The wedding coordinator, who has been hovering all evening, approaches him, crouching down next to his chair to be at eye-level.

"Mr. Page? Hi, I'm Leah. I just wanted to make sure you didn't need anything at all." She looks at the glass in front of him. "More water? Something else? Dinner will be served soon."

"Thank you, my dear. Your team has been very kind to me tonight."

"Of course." She smiles. "That's what we're here for. What can I get you?"

"Water is fine, thank you. Unless ... You haven't seen my granddaughter Karen, have you?"

"Sophie's mom? Well, let me think." Leah stands up. "No, I don't think so. Maybe at the bar right after the ceremony while Sophie was taking photos, but not since then."

"That is what I thought. Thank you all the same."

"Of course." She looks at him for another few seconds. "I'll get you some more water, sir."

And at once Marshall is sitting alone again. He feels like there is a big, black wall between him and his family. Or one of those two-way mirrors. He's completely detached from them, watching Ryan enjoy his wedding day without actually feeling like he is part of it.

He wants to go home, but he knows going home would solve nothing. He would feel just as disconnected there.

Leah returns with a bottle of water. "Would you like me to open it for you?"

Marshall looks down at his hands, weak and arthritic. "Yes. Thank you, dear."

She smiles at him as she breaks the seal on the lid and places the bottle in front of him. "One of my team will bring you dinner in just a minute, sir. You'll be okay alone?"

He nods and as she walks away he returns his attention to fiddling with the place card.

7:35pm Sophie

SOPHIE LEAVES the dining room where the photographers sit eating and continues looking in all the rooms on the ground floor of the house. She thinks it is after 7:30 sometime, because that's when they are supposed to eat dinner. Ryan had told her. But now everyone else is eating and she can't find her mom and she's really hungry.

She could probably get food without her, but then Mom would be hungry. Where is she?

Sophie continues down the hallway that runs the center of the first floor. There are a couple living areas in addition to the dining room she has already seen. Finally, near the end of the hallway, Sophie finds a closed door. She tries the handle. Locked.

"Someone in here!" a male voice calls through the door.

Maybe it's a bathroom? She thinks she hears another noise, and leans closer to the door. Muffled laughter.

There's another person in there. So, I guess it's not a bathroom? Sophie thinks. *That's weird.*

She waits very quietly for another minute and hears very faint giggling. Weird.

But that doesn't help her find her mom.

Sophie is really hungry.

She walks back down the length of the hallway, back to the kitchen. Aunt Callie stands in the doorway leading back outside. She smiles with relief when she sees Sophie. "There you are! Have you seen your mom? No? Well, no matter. Come on, we have a seat for you! Let's get you some dinner."

7:40pm Ian

THEY'RE MISSING DINNER. Ian can hear the chattering and the clinking of silverware through the tiny window.

The door handle jiggles. Someone's trying to open it.

"Someone in here!" he calls through the locked door. Karen giggles, leaning forward to bury her face in his neck.

There are no more attempts at the door, so Ian turns his focus back to the task at hand.

After that photographer bitch had blown him off, Ian ran into Karen at the bar again. She obviously had been waiting for him there. Drink in hand, leaning on the edge of the bar off to the side, irritating the bartender because she kept standing in front of his tip jar.

It had only taken another drink and some very extravagant flattery for them to now be locked in this bathroom with his hand up her tiny dress. Ian has taken off his tux jacket and thrown it over the toilet tank, but it's slipped to the floor. Karen has hopped up on the counter, legs spread, and pulled him to her.

This Karen girl is already pretty drunk. Enough that she's more than game for this, but not so much that he'll have to hold back her hair. The perfect amount, really. Plus, she's hot. The kind of hot that exudes experience and ease. The sexiness of confidence, even as she falls into the messy drunk phase.

"Shhhh…" she stage whispers, unbuttoning his pants. At the same time, her lips kiss his neck, down to his clavicle where she has already loosened his tie and collar.

Ian grins and echoes her. "Shhhh…" he says, reaching for his wallet and the condom inside before his pants drop to the floor.

Ten sweaty minutes later, Karen examines herself in the mirror and blots her face with a wad of toilet paper.

"Damn, it's hot in here."

Ian's naked butt sits on the cold edge of the tub, while he watches her. She's almost fully clothed still; only her purple, sheer, extremely tiny panties lay on the floor. Karen had bothered to remove her dress or even her shoes.

"So, what are you doing after this? Want to grab a drink or something?"

She turns to face him and the look she gives his amused pity. He feels her condescension. She leans forward and kisses him hard.

"Oh, sweetie." She lightly pats him twice on the cheek. "There's no 'after this.' Let's just leave it at this."

"What? Why?"

"It was fun. You're good. Don't worry. Just this, though, 'kay?" She turns back to the mirror, dismissing him and blotting her cleavage.

"Yeah, it was fun. So why not later?"

"Ian." She turns to look at him again. "I have a daughter. An eight-year-old little girl. You want me to bring her with?"

"Oh, no. You're right." Ian thinks for another moment. "What about tomorrow, then? Can you get a babysitter?"

"No, I gotta work."

"What about next weekend, then? Does your daughter ever go to her dad's?" Ian realizes he is being a little nosy but he doesn't care. He wants to see this girl again. Woman. Goddamn, she is some woman.

"I dunno, hon'. We'll see. Give me your number and I'll let you know."

"Yeah, ok," Ian mumbles. He takes her phone and dials his number. "It's the eight-one-eight number I just dialed."

While she finishes straightening her hair and reapplying her lipstick, Ian saves the missed call as 'Karen'. He could call her, he supposes. Even though he gets the feeling she doesn't want him to.

He is kind of surprised that he hasn't made a lasting impression in the last fifteen minutes. He has been told that he's very good.

Well, I still have the rest of the night, he thinks.

"You'll leave first?" she asks.

8:04pm Amber

AMBER SITS ALONE at the head table. She has taken off her shoes under the table; the grass is cool on her feet and is helping counter the heat from the day. The sun has set, but she still feels the fine coat of sticky sweat from the heat of the ceremony. She fiddles with the dessert fork that is still sitting in front of her, turning it over and over while she looks around at the guests.

All of the rest of the wedding party has eaten quickly and left again to go get another drink, talk to family sitting across the yard or, in many of the girls' cases, change into better shoes.

Dinner is just about over when she notices Ian emerge from the house. His mouth seems to be stained a little more pink than she had remembered. Is that lipstick? His face is impassive — whatever he had just been doing appears to have not moved him in the least.

The flower girl's mom emerges shortly after him, straightening her skirt.

Amber lets out an inadvertent snort. What a jackass.

What a selfish, insensitive jackass. First he takes advantage of her last night (yes, she let him. But still). Then he abuses the photographer, a total stranger. And now this? Does he have any substance at all? Is there anything even remotely redeeming about Ian McKay?

Amber rests her head on her arms, closing her eyes against the whole celebration. This is all just further evidence that last night had been the worst idea she has ever had. At least she can blame her puffy, crying eyes on the wedding.

The DJ turns up the volume on "Twist and Shout." Amber looks around; only the older guests are still seated. Well, and her. She's annoyed that the party can continue without her, and then angry at herself for being ridiculous. Of course it's going to go on whether she feels like partying or not.

A teenage boy in all black is standing just behind her.

"Excuse me, can I take that plate?" Amber looks up and he sees her eyes. "Oh, I'm so sorry. Are you ok?"

"Yeah." She shakes her head. "I'm sorry. I'm just … You know how there's those people in your life that would be great if they just changed that one thing about themselves?"

The waiter looks exasperated. "Yes. I totally do."

"I just realized he's never going to change." She sighs. "Never. This is just the way he is. And if I like him, I'm going to have to like him like this. You know?"

He looks up, over her shoulder at someone behind her. "I guess."

"Trust me. What are you? Fifteen? Just … save yourself the trouble now. Decide to love them the way they are or don't waste your time." Amber stands up, pushing her chair back.

8:15pm Dylan

DYLAN CARRIES the maid of honor's plate, along with all the other mostly empty dishes he's cleared from her table, and walks back to the catering truck. She had been sitting with her head on her arms on the table, her hair almost in the cream sauce left over from her chicken. Sitting all alone, while the rest of the wedding party was ... what? Dancing? Drinking? Clearly having more fun than she was, so he took pity on her and bussed the table. But now there are more guests on the dance floor than at the tables, so he can start clearing other dishes.

Dylan seeks his boss, Cheryl, and finds her behind the truck, directing one of the waitresses in stacking containers.

"You think it is okay to start clearing?" he asks, gesturing to the empty plate in his hand.

She barely glances at him before agreeing. "Yes, yes. I trust you. You're fine. Go ahead."

Dylan weaves his way between a couple other waiters, also packing things up, slips behind a group of guests standing in the walkway and makes his way to an abandoned table. His mom is near the house, taking to the DJ. She is just all business all the time. It makes her good at her job, sure, but is that all there is? Is there really no other way she can think to spend her energy?

He thinks about what the maid of honor had said, about caring about someone the way they are or not wasting your time. Could he love his mom this way? This controlling, cold, driven way that she is?

Out of the corner of his eye, Dylan sees a white blur head toward his mother. It's the bride, going out of her way to hug her wedding coordinator. He stops to watch for just a moment before returning to work. The bride is gushing; she repeatedly clasps his mom's arm. He is too far away to hear what is being said, but the way she keeps leaning into Leah as she talks feels intimate. Like she genuinely loves and values this hired help.

She is just a wedding coordinator — a glorified manager. And she inspires this much affection?

Dylan turns away to clear the next table, biting the inside of his cheek.

8:28pm Leah

LEAH HOVERS along the edge of the dance floor, one eye on the DJ, one eye on the serving staff, one eye on the photographer. Yes, that's three eyes. Leah is very good at her job. She pulls out her phone and glances at it — 8:28pm. An hour and a half left and still no word from Joe. Before she can return the phone to her pocket, her arm is pinned against her side in a tight hug.

"Oh my god, Leah. This has been amazing! You are my new best friend." Lindsay clutches Leah to her.

"Oh!" Leah has only been taken by surprise with the hug; she is used to brides declaring their undying love for her by the ends of their wedding days. "Of course, Lindsay. I'm so glad."

"No. I mean it." Lindsay pulls back but keeps a tight grip on Leah's shoulders. "I can't wait till Amber gets married so we get to work with you again!"

"Thank you." Leah can't help but grin.

"Is there anything I can do for you? I mean, I'll refer everyone I know, but would a testimonial help? Or a Yelp review?"

"Yes. Thank you so much, dear. But, please don't worry about me. Go enjoy your wedding. We can talk next week."

Lindsay hugs her again. "Thank you," she whispers into Leah's hair.

She watches the bride dash off into the crowd on the dance floor with Ryan close behind. He's helping hold up her enormous train, grinning as Lindsay spins and gets tangled in the yards of fabric.

Leah sighs. Joe used to be like that. Thoughtful and caring. Nurturing. He still is, to be honest. He will probably leave the porch light on for her when she gets home, looking out for what is best for her.

Which is why she knows that this separation — she is not ready to call it a divorce — is the best decision, as well. She sees that now. They need space. They need to make individual lives and see how that works. She has invested so much into her business, and now she needs to decide if she is willing to invest just as much into her marriage.

She tucks her phone back into the pocket of the tote bag, turning her full attention to the wedding.

8:45pm Kristy

KRISTY CHECKS HER PHONE AGAIN. 8:45pm Just over an hour left. Thank god. She is so done with this day.

Leah catches her eye from across the dance floor. Kristy feels guilty for a second, since she had been caught checking the time, until she sees Leah mouthing the work 'cake,' raising her eyebrows in a question, and pointing over to the cake table.

Got it. A bit of the many instances of sign language and secret messages sent between vendors on a wedding day. And Leah can think Kristy only has eyes for her beloved schedule.

Threading her way through the crowd of watchers surrounding the dance floor, Kristy keeps one eye out for Ian and one eye out for Marta. The cake table is over on the other side of the yard, so she imagines she'll run into one or both before she gets over there.

The cake is a lovely, simple traditional three-tier white confection adorned delicately with fresh flowers. Marta had been able to get some photos earlier, just before the ceremony when they still had plenty of natural light. As she approaches, Kristy notices that sometime in the last hour, a small plate, two forks and several napkins have found their way to the cake table.

She had seemed a bit distracted earlier, but Leah never misses anything, apparently.

The cake table is set up in the corner of the yard. No one has noticed her over there yet so Kristy takes the opportunity to really survey the scene. The backyard really does look beautiful. It's the perfect spot for a wedding. Small holiday lights are strung between the eaves of the house and the trees that pepper the yard. All of the tables feature centerpieces of candles, most of which remain lit casting a warm glow over the guests. There are several tables of grandparents and other older guests, strategically placed as far away from the DJ's speakers as possible. Ryan and Lindsay stand with a group of guests their own age — sorority sisters, maybe — laughing and completely ignoring the fact that Leah is trying to get their attention to keep them on schedule. Marta makes her way over to that corner of the yard and, at the bar —

Ian stares at her. He is clearly watching her. She holds his gaze for only a moment (*yes, I see you and I am ignoring you*) before looking away. She hopes he can feel her contempt, but his expression is blank. She can feel her face blushing; why is he looking at her? Thank god it is after dark. There are not many lights outside of the dance floor, and she doesn't think anyone else is looking at her.

She wills herself to not pull up on the neckline of her tank top. Intellectually, she knows she looks fine and that everything is covered. She knows that. She has to tell herself three times, but she knows it. It's only that she knows that pig is still looking at her that brings on the impulse. As a compromise, she tries to casually hold her big camera up in front of her chest. That looks natural, right? Is he still looking at her?

Goddamn that guy.

Goddamn this whole job.

She never wants to be put in this situation ever again. She supposes she could have held to her contract and left, but this is a wedding day. This day is never going to happen again. And it isn't Ryan and Lindsay's fault their brother is a revolting human being. But that is more than she ever wants to put herself through again.

Marta appears at her elbow.

"Hey," Kristy says. "They're supposed to be doing the cake right now. And then I assume the DJ will rush through the bouquet toss, garter toss and money dance before we leave at ten."

"Ok! Sounds good! I don't mind staying a little bit if we have to."

"I do. My husband is going to have our hot tub ready when I get home. I cannot wait to get out of here."

8:53pm Amber

THE PHOTOGRAPHER KRISTY approaches Amber as she stands at the edge of the dance floor. Before she can say anything, Amber smirks and points to what she is watching. Kristy follows her gaze.

The awkward DJ has brought out a little step stool, set it up in the middle of the dance floor and climbed up on to it. He is now at least four or five feet higher than the guests. He pulls out a small point-and-shoot camera, holds it high above the dance floor, and takes a single photo with a bright flash pointing almost straight down at the guests. Finally, he climbs down off the step stool, moves it to another spot and repeats the process.

"What is he doing?" Kristy laughs and Amber can't help but join her.

"I can only assume he is taking photos for his website?"

"What is it he thinks I do?"

Amber laughs again, totally confused. "I have no idea."

"Anyway. I was just coming over to see if you, Miss Maid of Honor, know about any bouquet toss surprises."

"What do you mean? Like what?"

"Oh, some brides have multiple ones to throw. Some turn

and look so they can throw it directly to someone. Things like that."

"No, Lindsay hasn't told me anything like that. Sorry."

Kristy shrugs. "It's fine. It doesn't really matter. I just thought I'd check. Actually, I'm kind of surprised she is doing a bouquet toss at all. There doesn't seem to be very many single women here tonight."

"No, there's not," replies Amber. She can probably count them all on one hand, actually. Including herself.

"Oh well."

Amber feels the other woman looking at her carefully.

"Are you okay?"

Amber stares at her for just a beat before replying. "Me? Yeah, of course. I mean… It's a wedding! I'm happy."

She looks at Amber, politely skeptical. She nods, seeming to accept Amber's words at face value.

"Ok. Good."

Amber wonders what she sees. Are her eyes still red and puffy? It's kind of dark in the backyard, with only strands of bulbs offering ambient light. Had she maybe heard about Amber's tangle with Ian? Ironically, Amber is feeling semi-alright. Now that it's the end of the day and someone has finally thought to notice she might be having a hard time. She can actually say she's fine and have it mostly be true.

"Actually, I think it's time for the bouquet toss — it must be almost nine o'clock." Kristy indicates over to the dance floor with a slight tilt of her heard.

At that exact moment, the DJ starts playing "All the Single Ladies."

"Alright, you know what that means! I want to see all the single ladies out on the dance floor for the bouquet toss!"

Kristy rolls her eyes. "Ah yes. So predictable. Excuse me."

9:42pm Sophie

THE WEDDING IS PROBABLY ALMOST OVER. ALREADY a few of her great-aunts and uncles have left. But most of the people Sophie's mom's age are still here. Dancing, mostly, just like Sophie.

Sophie loves this song — it's one that she and her mom dance too sometimes in the car. Not really at home. Mom isn't usually in the mood to listen to music when she's home. But sometimes, like on the way to the grocery store or when Sophie is going to be dropped off at her dad's, Mom puts this song on. They both know all the words. Where is her mom now? Sophie tries to look around while she dances, but she doesn't notice anyone wearing the same bright color of her mom's dress.

Sophie is dancing with one of the boys. One of cousin Ryan's friends that stood up at the front with him. He had worn sunglasses during the wedding, which Sophie thought was so cool.

"Hey Soph!" Uncle Tory grabs her hand and starts swinging her arm from side to side in time with the music. "Ready to go home? It's already almost ten, way past your bedtime. I think

Aunt Callie is asking your mom if you can come stay with us tonight."

"Ok." Sophie had spent all day waiting for her mom to have time for her, and now she isn't even going home with her. She tries to smile at Uncle Tory. So he knows she's happy. Even though she's not happy.

She feels sharp fingers on her arm. "Come on, Sophie. Let's go."

Her mom is angry. She can tell. She almost pulls Sophie off her feet as she starts toward the edge of the dance floor, back towards the front of the house. The boy who had been wearing the sun glasses stays where he is in the middle of the crowd, but Uncle Tory follows behind Sophie and her mom.

"Karen, hey. Karen," he calls after them. "Did Callie find you?"

"Yeah, she fucking found me." Mom whirls around. The small group of other guests talking nearby collectively step back, away from where her mom is yelling. "Told me I couldn't take care of my daughter. You keep that bitch away from me." She turns back around and continues dragging Sophie toward the driveway.

Sophie tries to make herself go small. When her mom gets mad like this, the best thing to do is hope she doesn't notice you. Mom still has a tight grip on her arm, but if she can keep in step and move closer to her mom the grip will relax and Sophie can feel her attention slide right off of her.

"Hey. Wait. Karen, wait!"

She turns around again to confront her brother, fuming.

"Karen, we just thought you seemed to be having fun and we'd take the girl home so you could keep having fun. I swear!" He puts up his hands like he's warding her off. "We didn't mean anything by it. If you don't want her to come with us, she won't."

Aunt Callie had found them now and watches the conversation, her lips pursed. Sophie tries not to smile too big. Her mom *does* want to be with her. They're going to go home together. Right now, even. Mom even got mad at Uncle Tory for wanting to take her instead. Sophie bites her lip. She doesn't want to hurt Uncle Tory's feelings. She looks down so he can't see her smile.

"Karen," Aunt Callie says. "Look. We love Sophie. We love you. We're just trying to help. It's been a long day for everyone. We can bring Sophie back to our place so she can get a full night's sleep and you can … you know. Continue doing whatever you want to do."

"Fuck you," Mom spits out. "Whatever I 'want to do'? Fuck you. You don't know me."

"Karen, shut up."

"Callie, don't — "

"No, she needs to listen. We do everything we can for Sophie. We are *always* available to babysit at a last minute notice. We go out of our way to help her out. And now? Now that it actually seems *dangerous* to leave Sophie with her we're just going to step aside?"

"Callie —"

"Karen, you are a disaster. You are a walking time bomb. I lost track of how many drinks you had tonight — you should *not* be driving at all, let alone with your eight-year-old daughter."

Sophie's mom glares at Aunt Callie. About five or six guests are leaving at the same time, but give Sophie's family a wide berth. No one wants to interfere. Sophie just wants it to be over. She has never heard Aunt Callie this angry, but she has seen her mom like this. It never goes well.

"Give me your keys." Aunt Callie holds out her hand.

Sophie's mom snorts derisively and turns away. She puts her arm around Sophie's shoulders and forcibly propels her forward toward the street, away from the wedding. Away from her brother and the rest of her family.

Uncle Tory calls after them, but her mom ignores them.

Sophie looks back over her shoulder. Only briefly, though.

She has to concentrate on keeping up with her mom as she is half-dragged down the driveway to their car. Uncle Tory and Aunt Callie are watching them, his arm around her shoulders. They both look sad. Sophie faces front again, without waving good-bye.

Her mom says nothing as they get into the car.

A LOT of the older guests are leaving. Once the cake has been served, there is not a whole lot left to hang around for. Ian had been dancing with Sophie, before she was pulled away. She is a cute kid, sure. But really he had just been trying to get Karen's attention. She has not left yet — she's talking to her brother and his girlfriend just on the edge of the dance floor — so Ian thinks there might be a chance. Not tonight, and not tomorrow, but he wants some kind of indication that she wants to see him again.

He gets slightly jostled as someone passes. Amber is walking across the dance floor, purse over her shoulder, carrying her heels and walking barefoot. She doesn't look right or left, or give any notice to anyone.

"Hey hey hey," he calls after her. She's leaving without even saying good-bye? "You leaving? You want to go get a drink or something?"

She stops and watches him as he jogs toward her. "Um. No, thank you. I just want to go home."

"You want a ride?" He grins.

"No, Ian. Please, just … I'm really tired. I'll see you some other time. Good-bye."

"Wait wait. I thought last night was fun?" He lowers his voice to his 'just us' level and tries to put his hand on her waist to pull her closer but she side steps his touch.

"Well, for a while it was fun. But ... Ian." She looks at him with the same pity he saw in Karen's face. "That was a one-time thing, okay?"

"What? C'mon, Amber. We're great together. Why are you blowing me off?"

She heaves a big sigh and stands quietly for a few moments.

"What?"

"Ian. I don't really know how to say this without making it sound rude. So, I guess I'll just say it?"

He narrows his eyes, but doesn't respond.

"You're ..." She rolls her eyes, but makes herself continue. "You're very handsome. And very charming. And you are a really great kisser."

He grins. "Yeah?"

"Don't interrupt."

They eye each other.

"But, Ian ... I mean. I'm sorry, but there's not much more to you." She winces a little as she says it.

"What?" He tries hard not to come off offended. To sound nonchalant. An uninterested bystander. He can't overreact. He knows she'll stop telling him what he needs to hear if she thinks he's going to flip out.

"Ian, I have known you more than half your life, right? Since you were... what? Seven or eight? You used to be this adorably sweet kid who liked basketball and LEGOs, remember? And then somewhere along the line you hit puberty and got obnoxious. You discovered girls and you have never been the same."

"So? I'm a guy. I grew up. What's the problem?"

Amber sighs and looks around. They're still on the dance floor. "I don't really think that now is the time or place to get into all of it, Ian."

"What the fuck, then? You just blow me off and don't tell me why? Except that I don't like LEGOs anymore?" He grabs her elbow and pulls her around to the far side of the dance floor as he says this, in the shadows of the house.

"Okay okay." Amber covers her face with her hands, rubbing her eyes. "Ian, you know that I care about you. As Lindsay's brother. I'm not trying to hurt you, but … "

"But, what, Amber? Fuck, just spit it out."

She sighs, finally looking him directly in the eyes. "Since you discovered girls… you haven't really been interested in anything else."

"So?" Why was she making this so difficult? She wasn't making any sense.

"So … I'm not interested in girls. Karen isn't interested in girls. But you are interested in nothing else. Which means you and I have nothing in common. You see?"

He frowns, trying to follow.

"You're not the kind of guy who is good for more than a couple dates. There is literally nothing for us to talk about. You're just not meant to be a boyfriend. And there are very few girls who are going to hook up with you more than once or twice since there is clearly no future with you."

Ian is stunned.

Amber continues, talking a little faster now that the worst is over. "But, Ian, you're young. This is probably just a phase, right? And then you'll mature a little and live the rest of your life happy in a longer-than-two-nights relationship."

This is too much. "Fuck you. I'm twenty-two."

"Oh. Well, excuse me," she says. "Yes, my mistake. The wisdom of all your many years has surely solved this problem."

"Fuck you," he mutters.

She throws up her hands. "Fine. Nevermind. You've got it all under control." Amber rubs her temple again. "I'll see ya."

She reaches for his hand, squeezing it just once before dropping it and walking away.

Ian wants nothing more than to punch something or some-one. But, as there is nothing nearby but the wall of the house he forces himself to calm down.

I should just go home, he thinks. *I can't drink any more here or I won't be able to drive. I'll go home and drink there.*

He looks up in time to see Karen and Sophie walking down the dark driveway a little bit ahead of Amber.

Damn it, he thinks. *Damn it, damn it.*

10:02pm Kristy

KRISTY LEANS against the side of the house, trying to take some of the weight off her feet. She's standing directly under the porch lamp. Lit from above, she can picture exactly how she looks with the harsh shadows cutting across her face. Her eyes must look hollow and her cheekbones dominating. She takes a deep breath and lets it out slowly as she rolls her shoulders back. The bruise she predicted has made its appearance where her camera bag has been hanging all day.

She pulls her phone out of the side pocket of the camera bag. 10:02pm. Thank God. She can pack up and leave. Go home. Kick her shoes off and crawl into bed. She has officially fulfilled her contract and no longer has to stand around watching slightly tipsy people dance atrociously.

A quick glance around tells her most of the guests have left. Lindsay, Ryan and a couple of the bridesmaids are still on the dance floor, but Amber is already almost to the end of the driveway. The flower girl has been taken home. The groomsman with the baby — what is his name — has left an hour ago. The wedding is definitely winding down, and Kristy won't miss anything.

Hell, even the bar has been packed up. Everyone has been cut off. The evening is done.

Marta is still on her feet — half-dancing, half-photographing the gorgeous twenty-something girls still dancing. All three of them have lost their shoes sometime in the last couple hours and are holding up their long gowns with one hand. The bottom hems of are probably ruined. At least dirty, maybe ripped.

Not that anyone ever really wears their bridesmaid dresses again.

"Last song for the lovebirds," the DJ croons. The first two iconic notes in Etta James's voice come through the speakers.

"My looooove has come along …" Marta has made her way over to Kristy and sings right next to her.

Kristy smiles. "It's a great song. You ready?"

"Sure thing. Let me just grab my bag from the dining room."

"Cool. I'm going to go say good-bye. Meet me back here."

Kristy hoists the camera bag back on to her shoulder — balanced perfectly on the bruise, of course. She'll take some Advil before she goes to bed tonight — and moves off to find the boss.

"Leah? Hey, I just wanted to let you know we're out of here. Great wedding."

Leah is sitting down for maybe the first time all day. The first time Kristy has seen her do it at least. The reception tables are all cleared of dishes, most of centerpieces and straggling party favors, and Leah is seated way back in the dark corner of the backyard where she will not be seen. But still, she is seated.

She stands when she hears Kristy call for her.

"Thank you so much for all your hard work today, Kristy."

"Of course. No problem. Just doing my job."

"I hope I see you again soon," Leah says, shaking her hand.

"Sure." Kristy smiles. "Maybe."

She makes her way back to where Marta is waiting. Everything is packed up. Everything ready to be taken home, away from this wedding. From any wedding.

"Ok. I'm ready. Let's go home!" Marta has her wide camera bag slung over her shoulder, water bottle in hand.

"At last." Kristy can't help but grin. The final notes peter out as they walk down the dark driveway.

10:09pm Dylan

DYLAN IS TAKING one last moment alone before heading home. The strings of bistro lights criss-crossing over the back-yard lend a warm glow to the entire event. But the driveway where he stands now is dark in contrast. Dark enough that he feels hidden, but not dark enough that he can see more than a small handful of stars. That would be unheard of this close to the city.

The grandpa from earlier comes to the end of the walkway, staring down the mostly dark driveway. He hasn't seemed like he has dementia when Dylan talked to him earlier, but maybe he does.

Dylan moves a couple steps closer — just enough into the light that he can be seen. He doesn't want to poor man to think he's being spied on.

"Oh, hello, my boy. I'm sorry. Can you tell me what time it is?"

"It's, uh, ten after or so."

"I see. And did you happen to see the woman I came with. Or her lovely daughter, the flower girl?"

Dylan thinks about who is left back on the dance floor. "No. I don't think so. Would you like me to check?"

"No, that's alright."

He is quiet for so long, Dylan almost walks away. But the man is … old. At least in his eighties. And apparently his family has forgotten him. Again. Dylan doesn't feel right just leaving him alone, in the dark without any way home.

"Can, uh… Can I help you with something, Mr. Page?"

He lets go a long, deep breath. "No, I don't think so. Unless you can call me a cab? I don't carry a cell phone, you see."

"Sure, of course." Dylan pulls out his phone and starts looking up a number.

"How much do you think a cab would be?"

"Oh…. Um. I'm sorry, sir. I have no idea. This is Los Angeles. I don't know if I've ever taken a cab in my life." He half laughs apologetically.

"Of course. You're right. Thank you." He turns back to look down the dark driveway.

Dylan thinks for a minute. About what his mother has always taught him about work ethic and about how this man doesn't seem to have any family interested in him. "Just one moment, Mr. Page. I'll be right back."

Dylan turns and runs, dodging the couple of guests still milling around and slipping passed the DJ's table to find his mom. She is in the back of the yard, staring at her phone while her team piles up folding chairs around her.

"Mom. Hey, mom!"

10:29pm Sophie

SOPHIE and her mom are almost home. There is always some traffic in Los Angeles, even on a Saturday night, but they are mostly lucky tonight. The clock on the dashboard reads 10:29pm. Way past Sophie's bed time.

"Did you have a good time, baby?"

"Yes, mom."

"I'm glad." She reaches over and squeezes Sophie's knee. "Did you make any new friends? I know I didn't see you a lot of the night."

"Kinda. Um … the photographer lady was nice to me. And that boy that wore the sunglasses during the wedding?" She giggles. "He danced with me. We danced to "Welcome to New York." He's not as good as you though, mom."

"Hey, that's our song."

Sophie grins. It has been so long since her mom had teased her. Or remembered their song.

"Let's listen to it, 'kay? Find my phone cord for me?"

Sophie pulls her mom's purse onto her lap from where it had been resting at her feet. The gray Corolla is already ten years old, so it takes a bit of tweaking and customizing to get to play any music from the phone to the stereo. But Sophie is an expert. She has done this many times before.

Sophie feels her body lean slightly to the right as her mom swerves the car unexpectedly. But she is focused on finding the right cord to plug in the phone so they can listen to the song.

Bright blue and red lights bounce into Sophie's eyes from the mirrors.

"Oh fuck," her mom says. "Fuck fuck fuck *fuck*. Oh shit. Ok. Here's what we're going to do."

Sophie freezes. What's happening? Mom pulls the car over to the side of the road. Before the car is even in park, she snatches her purse from Sophie's lap and begins frantically pawing through it.

"Okay, Sophie. I don't know what is going to happen, but I need you to make sure you grab your jacket. Got it? Good." She pops an Altoid into her mouth and continues to talk around it. "And take my phone so you can call your dad. Looks like it needs to be charged, so don't use it until you have to. If you can't reach Dad call Uncle Tory, ok?"

Sophie nods, crying. Why would she need to call Dad? She feels like she might be sick.

A tall, stern man — is that a policeman's uniform? — walks up to her mom's side of the car and taps on the window.

10:35pm Amber

ONCE AGAIN ALONE, Amber fishes her apartment keys out of her purse. The security light by her door had burned out a couple days earlier, but it has been replaced sometime since she had left. Even with the bright new bulb, she has to stab at the handle three times before she can find the hole and slip the key in. She carries only her purse and her shoes. Her overnight bag, with two days worth of clothes, her make-up, even her tooth-brush is still in the car. All of that can wait until tomorrow.

The straps of her black heels are hooked just barely in her pinky while she tries to hang on to her keys and turn the door handle at the same time. She drops all of it on the floor just inside the door as soon as she takes a step in. Her purse gets tossed onto the entry way table, right by where her keys are *supposed* to go. She closes the door behind her with just her foot. She will lock it up in a second.

Amber drags her feet the final six or seven steps and collapses into her wide armchair.

She has not been home since Friday morning — almost forty-eight hours — and is so glad she had the forethought to clean a bit before she left. There is nothing better than coming home to a cleared off table, soap-smelling bathroom, and clean carpet under her feet.

Her head aches from the bobby pins, and she feels like she has a fine layer of dirt all over her. She probably does. A whole day's worth of dirt and sweating.

What a day.

Amber thinks back to the shower she had had that morning. Such a lovely quiet time before having to spend an entire day pretending to be happy and not miserably lonely.

She grabs the arms of the chair and hoists herself back to standing. With one hand she locks her front door, turns out the living room lamp and with the other hand continues to pull out bobby pins, collecting quite the pile as she makes her way to the bathroom.

Amber roots around in the bottom drawer of the vanity while the shower water heats up. There — found it. A new bar of luxury soap from Lush. Sandstone. She had bought this for herself for her last birthday and had been saving this for a special occasion. No day like today.

The mirror is already beginning to fog up when she steps into the tub. Amber begins immediately to massage her scalp, wetting her hair and scratching her nails across the more tender areas where bobby pins had been lodged for ten hours. She closes her eyes, feeling the hot water massage her neck and back, washing away the grime from the day. Calming her anxiety, even, and giving her yet another fresh start.

Amber takes a deep breath as she rubs the sweet, slightly citrus soap against her skin, exfoliating and helping her lose the layer of wedding day covering her surface and have a fresh clean start.

10:39pm Ian

THE CLOCK on the dashboard says 10:39 when Ian parks his car. His parents aren't home yet; they hadn't looked like they were even close to leaving when Ian said good-bye at the wedding.

Well, at least someone enjoyed it, he thinks.

The house is dark, but Ian leaves the lights off as he walks through the entryway. The dark feels friendlier somehow, like he can better think through this whole mess without the glare of light to push away his thoughts. In the kitchen, the bright light from the refrigerator is overwhelming. He has to stand there, letting his eyes adjust, for a moment before he grabs a beer.

Fuck. He is fucking alone on a Saturday night after spending all evening with tipsy bridesmaids. How is that even possible? What the fuck is wrong with him?

Is Amber right? Goddamn it, what if every girl thinks the same thing? Do they really think he is that big of a loser?

Ian finishes his beer standing right there in the kitchen, and grabs a second before heading back to his bedroom.

Ian realizes he could probably call Karen, or send a message to her through Ryan. If he wants to. But first, he needs to figure out what his problem is. How did he fuck up this weekend already after such a promising start?

Is Amber right? He keeps coming back to this thought. Is he really not worth more than a night or two? Do girls really see him like that? What is he interested in other than chasing pussy?

He wanders almost aimlessly through the door to his bedroom. It is full of dirty clothes all over the floor. He has a desk in the corner under the window where he used to do homework, but now it is just piled with dirty dishes and empty Red Bull cans. Ian stands in the middle of the room and does a full 360-degree rotation, looking all around him.

He keeps the light off, and uses the glow from his cell phone to step around the clothes on the floor.

He remembers when he used to have L.A. Lakers bed sheets. He remembers the Kobe Bryant posters and the little Nerf hoop that used to be hanging up. Even further back, he remembers spending entire Sundays in here building elaborate castles or space stations with LEGOs. But now?

Fuck, he thinks as he sinks onto the bed. He's not careful, and the beer in his hand sloshes out of the can onto his tux pants.

Oh well. He doesn't have anything else to do tomorrow except return the tux. They could get the beer out then.

He sits up straight, realizing: He doesn't have anything to do tomorrow. Because he doesn't have a girlfriend and doesn't have any hobbies. What the fuck?

Is Amber right?

He does another look around, but more slowly. There is nothing in this room that is interesting. He can finally see it through Amber's eyes. The guy who lives here is a tool. He has spent so long trying to be the cool guy who got girls that he has forgotten what it is that actually interests him.

Ian is not tired — it's not even eleven. He's used to staying up much later. So he might as well do something. He pulls out his laptop, settles back against his headboard and opens a new browser window. While the wifi connects, he pauses with his hands over the keys. Where does he want to go first? It is June, so the Finals are probably just over.

He types 'Lakers trade rumors' into Google and hits enter. He would start here and see if he could somehow find himself again.

10:48pm Kristy

KRISTY WALKS in her front door at ten till eleven. She had had to thread through the crowd to say good-bye to Lindsay and Ryan and wish them a happy honeymoon. Then she had that long walk down the driveway and across the street to where her car was. Then, of course, there was the regular Saturday night traffic on the 101. It was a long road home. At least Marta had parked at Kristy's house so she had not had to make another tour. Thank god Nick had been waiting at the door for her — he opens it as Marta's car pulls away.

"Hi, honey. How did it go? You okay?" He meets her on the front walk way to take her heavy camera bag from her and hand her a drink.

"Fine. I'll tell you all about it, but I need to do something online real quick before I go to bed."

"Ok! You go do that, put on your swimsuit. Or not. And I'll meet you out back?"

She smiles and kisses him. It's so nice to be home. He sets her camera bag just inside the door to her office and leaves her alone.

She needs it. She has been with a crowd of strangers all

night. Now is finally the time to be alone. Now that she has come to the moment of decision she needs to make this happen by herself. Nick only ever supports her choices, but this is something she needs to do without any input from anyone.

Kristy opens her laptop. Internet browser, the admin page of her website, and opens a new blank blog post.

The cursor blinks at her.

She is going to quit photography.

Not just weddings. All professional photography. Now that she is on the downhill side of this decision she can see clearly all the signs her body had been giving her, all the indications that she isn't really happy. Kristy does some quick calculations — she can't afford to back out of the weddings she has already booked so she would have to shoot them. Twelve more total.

She can do that. Just twelve more.

She can not wait to tell Nick. He will be happy if this makes her happy. She needs to tell him as soon as possible — otherwise she will talk herself out of it.

She takes a breath and starts typing: *I am so excited to announce my retirement from photographing weddings...*

As she writes out her announcement, Kristy feels the doubt receding. Putting this all in words is not only helping her clarify her thoughts, but also reminding her that she has completely valid reasons for stepping away from this business.

She rereads her words.

She slowly takes a breath. Kristy wants to feel the air all the way to the bottom of her lungs. She lets it out slowly as she hit 'publish'.

Once she confirms the information is out in the world, Kristy immediately closes her laptop and gets up from the desk. She will back up the photos tomorrow. If she stays on the computer she might give in to her second thoughts.

She will have to find some other career, but that can wait. Right now, her husband and the hot tub wait for her.

10:57pm Dylan

DYLAN OPENS the front door to find his mom slumped into the couch, groping for the television remote. She does not appear to be looking that hard, but she'll still never notice that it is on the floor next to her.

He crouches down to grab it for her and hands it over without saying a word. She gives him a grateful, teary smile before directing her attention to the gadget in her hand.

He stands behind the couch, and immediately notices that there are some framed photos missing from the top of the mantel. Not more than two or three, but his dad must have taken them. His only claim to their shard belongings — copies of photos that Mom probably has backed up digitally in four different places.

She punches the on button. Punches it again when the television doesn't respond quickly enough.

"Here, Mom. Let me help you."

He can navigate away from the Blu-Ray player and into the Netflix queue in as few clicks as possible. Something that would have taken her way too long. Now that he thinks about it, she may not have ever turned on the television since they got

Netflix. In literally years. He can't remember ever seeing her sit down to watch a movie without him or his dad around.

He cannot remember the last time he has seen her actually relax like this.

He's still standing behind her, but can see her wipe away a tear.

She needs him as much as Dad does.

Dylan squeezes his mom's hand and leaves her to her *Friends* marathon.

10:59pm Marshall

MARSHALL DROPS HIS KEYS. He tries to stifle his groan as he bends down to pick them up. At least the hallway is well lit.

As soon as the thought crosses his mind, the bulb closest to him flickers.

It's late. For Marshall, yes, but also for every other resident of this apartment complex. They all go to bed

They're all old. And living alone. Just like him.

Nevertheless, he tries to remain as quiet as possible as he lets himself inside and locks the door behind him. No point in ruining anyone else's evening.

Because his night had been ruined. He had woken up that morning looking forward to spending the afternoon and evening at a family wedding and had ended it up left behind and completely ignored by everyone who is supposed to love him the most.

The only people who had taken time to talk to him the entire night had been the staff. The hired help. The people who were being paid to be there. Not one member of his family had taken the time to sit down with him at all. Not any of his two kids, two kids-in-law or thirteen grandchildren. Sophie did, bless her heart. But Marshall wonders if even that would have happened if her mother had been more attentive.

He hurries to remove his clothes, get a glass of water and crawl into bed.

As he pulls the blankets up over him, Marshall looks at the clock. 10:59pm. He will be awake again in just a few hours.

On his nightstand, next to his book, is his bottle of sleeping pills. He has needed these pills nearly every night for at least a year. His doctor is understanding and kind, but refuses to increase his dosage.

His body is so tired, but he knows his brain won't give in.

He tips the plastic bottle, leaving two of the pills in his palm. He swallows them quickly with a single gulp of water and lies down.

Marshall loves his family. Of course. He doesn't deny that even to himself. But he honestly wonders sometimes how much they love him. How much they will really miss him when he is gone.

He sits up again to take two more pills. As late as it is, his mind is still racing and he needs the help to sleep.

He feels like he can't breathe. The pills will slow his racing heart and help him forget the day.

He has already taken is much more than the recommended dose, but Marshall just wants to sleep. He wants to turn off the thoughts in his head. He just wants it to end. He finishes all the pills that are in the bottle, taking the time to drink plenty of water to help them dissolve more quickly.

Marshall closes his eyes, willing the pills to work and release him from this day.

Free stories

_____

SIGN-UP AT AMYTEEGAN.COM/FREE for free short stories and reading recommendations.

Afterword

Thank you so much for reading *No Day Like Today*. If you loved the book, a review on your favorite retailer would help me out more than I can possibly tell you.

Thank you to that one drunk groomsman who was at the last wedding I ever photographed and without whom this book would not exist.

Thank you to all the wedding professionals who make these magical days happen.

Thank you to my author friends who helped and encouraged me at every step.

Thank you to my beta readers, especially Mike, for pushing me to get this book out.

Thank you to you, my reader, my new favorite person. I'm so glad you're here.

About the Author

Amy Teegan is a reader, writer and traveler living in Austin, Texas.

Follow her at amyteegan.com.

No Day Like Today is a work of fiction. Names, characters, places and incidents either are the product of the author's imagination or are used fictitiously. Any resemblance to actual persons living or dead, events or locales is entirely coincidental.

Copyright 2018 by Amy Teegan

Cover art by Okay Creations

All rights reserved.

No part of this publication may be reproduced, distributed, or transmitted in any form or by any means, including photocopying, recording or other electronic or mechanical methods, without the prior written permission of the publisher, except in the case of brief quotations embodied in critical reviews and certain other noncommercial uses permitted by copyright law.

 Created with Vellum

www.ingramcontent.com/pod-product-compliance
Lightning Source LLC
Chambersburg PA
CBHW050849180626
46814CB00007B/2699